SUMMER OF THE DRUMS

Also by Theodore V. Olsen

BREAK THE YOUNG LAND

THE STALKING MOON

BITTER GRASS

ARROW IN THE SUN

EYE OF THE WOLF

THERE WAS A SEASON

Summer of the Drums

THEODORE V. OLSEN

DOUBLEDAY & COMPANY, INC.

GARDEN CITY, NEW YORK

1972

ISBN: 0-385-05694-X
Library of Congress Catalog Card Number 72–79413
Copyright © 1972 by Theodore V. Olsen
All Rights Reserved
Printed in the United States of America
First Edition

To Diane, Neal, and Rob

AUTHOR'S NOTE

Of the people who appear in this book, the following really lived: Zachary Taylor, Jefferson Davis, Hercules Dousman, Captain Samuel McRee, Captain Joseph Throckmorton, and Black Hawk. All others are fictitious. The story itself, though laid against a background of actual events, is entirely fictitious. Several time aspects of the Black Hawk War have been slightly altered for purposes of the story.

SUMMER OF THE DRUMS

CHAPTER ONE

"Ben, I want you to hold the craft steady."

Benjamin and Theron had been clowning in the back of the canoe, swiping water at each other with their short cedar paddles. Pa, sitting up in the prow, spoke without raising his voice or turning his head. But they both stopped fooling around directly and put their paddles to a proper use. Not that Ben didn't usually tend to business, as he had to, being steersman. But Theron always had ants in his britches and could never stay quiet for long.

Pretty soon I felt a cold dribble of water down my back. Theron was holding his dripping paddle over my neck. "Quit it, Ther," I said, raising my paddle. "I'll bust you square in the mouth."

"Don't get your hocks in an uproar, ole timer."

I looked back. Theron grinned wide to split, lifting his big hand palm open. I knew what the gesture meant: that he'd get me alone first chance and peel down my pants and spank the tar out of me. He'd been doing it for as long as I could remember and it was pretty humiliating that he still could, though I was fifteen and he topped me by less than three years.

He shook his paddle, flipping drops in my face. Mad as a hen, I dashed a handful of water at him. Snap, our elkhound, curled his tail over his back and leaped up on a pile of cargo, barking wildly.

"Now belay that!" Pa roared. "Next thing one of you'll be overboard. Or you'll get the furs wet, worse luck."

Snap's tail sank like a limp sausage, and he tried to hunker out of sight. Pa had swung his head to profile now, and we could see one wintry blue eye and his jutting beard. Just for a second or so. But it kept all of us mute as mice for the next half hour and a good two miles of strong paddling.

The May morning was crisp and sunny. Red-winged blackbirds rustled in the reeds along the riverbanks, and a fragrance of hepatica and arbutus drifted off the prairie slopes. It had been a fairly mild winter, as Northwest winters went. But a long, hard one for all of us. We'd been up and out every murky dawn, following our traplines all day, tramping the bogs and wading the thin-crusted creeks, picking up our catches and resetting the traps. At night we'd stumble home after dark exhausted and half frozen, wolf down the hot supper Mother and Ena had ready, and spend the evening skinning carcasses and stretching hides on hoop frames. Before the snow was half off the ground we'd been out plugging sugar maples to catch the sap run, and it seemed right on the heels of that came the spring plowing. Of course, there was plenty to keep us occupied between these seasonal jobs. The stock had to be cared for, wood cut and hauled and then sawed and chopped to fire size.

Pa not only held that idle hands were the devil's playpen, he was a stickler for education. Times you had to rest and just wanted to toast your toes by the fire, he or Mother were catching us up on our three R's and then some. We'd brought along plenty of books when we'd made the move from Massachusetts to Michigan Territory six years ago.

The Trasks had all been Boston bluebloods till Pa had broken the mold and run away to sea when he was no older than me. Later he had been a schoolteacher, then a government surveyor for a time, and he'd been on Commodore Perry's flagship at the Battle of Lake Erie in 1813. He had turned farmer after he'd married Mother, but he'd never outgrown the itch in his foot. You'd never guess that restless side of him unless you knew. Pa was big as a western grizzly, topping six feet four in his sock feet, and his blond hair was going to gray. He was usually stern and austere and didn't talk much except to give orders.

New country, new prospects. The wilderness had to be opened, and the young United States had to expand. Pa had deep feelings about such things, but for us three boys the growing-up years on our remote farm on the Blue River, miles from anywhere, had just been a boy's idea of paradise. Hard as we worked, there was time for hunting, fishing, roaming the woods. It couldn't have been such a great life for Mother or our sister Rowena, but they never complained.

In this spring of 1832, the half of Michigan Territory west of Lake Michigan was still four years from being declared the Territory of Wisconsin. The only real settlement was in the southeast corner, where the lead-mining country of Illinois and the Trans-Mississippi overlapped into Michigan. The first Yankee settlers like us were starting to farm the area, and the French-Canadian *voyageurs* and trappers still roamed the region as they had for two hundred years, bringing their furs to trade at John Jacob Astor's post in Prairie du Chien above the mouth of the Wisconsin River.

"Pa, we ought to raise Prairie pretty quick," Ben called from the stern.

"Close," Pa said. "Leclerc's Ferry is just ahead."

As he spoke, we swept around a wide bend of the Wisconsin and saw Leclerc's stone house and flat-bottomed Ferry on the north bank. Ben and Theron and me let out whoops and plied our paddles. Less than two miles on, the Mississippi River unfolded before us like a sun-wrinkled sheet. It was broad and blue, and patched with tan silt from the heavy thaw water. We swung out of the Wisconsin confluence and shot our *canot du nord* into a backwater slough between the wooded islands, heading upriver toward Prairie du Chien.

Ben and Theron put their backs into it, whooping from time to time, both of them excited as kids. At twenty, Ben was Pa's size, bull-big and just as blond, his fair skin tanned like fine leather. Theron had his full growth at eighteen and he wasn't so hefty, but he was nearly as tall and strong. Neither of them was much like Pa except physically; they were a boisterous pair, always funning. But different too. Ben was like a deep current that moves slow and deliberately; he had a wide, easy grin and a booming laugh. Ther was dark like Mother and me, quick and nervous, his moods darting like fish, and he was always up to something.

And there was me. Kevin Trask. The runt of the family. I guess you'd say I was middling size for my age, but thin and wiry, and always conscious of being the shrimp beside Pa and my brothers. I felt ferociously set on plenty of times by Theron, and it wasn't much comfort that Ben always took my part if Ther's prodding turned too rough. "Why don't you leave the kid alone?" he'd say. And it wouldn't be a request.

Prairie du Chien was coming into sight on the Mississippi's east bank. It was an old French town that the *voyageurs* had named long ago. Finding a village of Fox Indians on the site and learning the chief's name was Alim, meaning "dog," they'd called the spot "Plain of the Dog"—Prairie du Chien. After the British had taken over New France, they had built up the fur trade here until the Revolution, but the town was still three-quarters made up of French-speaking people of mixed white and Indian blood. Part of the village was on an offshore island where the Astor post stood. On the main shore was Fort Crawford, four fine stone buildings enclosing a parade ground, and scattered around it were a few log houses and some Winnebago lodges. These crude structures housed the brigades of *engagés*, trappers employed by the American Fur Company, and their families.

We pulled our big "north canoe" into the Marais de St. Feriole, the long slough dividing the island from the shore. It was a regular beehive this time of year. The waterfront was crowded with keelboats and flatboats, *bateaux* and canoes. Hunters were in from the West with loads of buffalo hides, and dozens of *coureur de bois*, free trappers, had arrived with their winter's cache of furs. White and Indian trappers alike would get a fair shake from the Astor agent, "King Joe" Rolette, and his partner Hercules Dousman, but they could expect no mercy from the sharp-nosed traders up from St. Louis with boatloads of blankets, guns, traps, trinkets, and whisky.

An Army officer was pacing back and forth along the dock, hands clasped behind him, watching the activity. Ben raised his paddle. "Hello, Colonel!" he boomed.

Colonel Zachary Taylor smiled, surveying our twenty-foot craft and its occupants. Pa bulking in the prow, our cache of furs amidships with Snap tail-wagging on top, me and Ther and Ben toward the back. "Now I know it's spring," he said. "Trasks popping up like crocuses. How are you, Amos?"

"Middling, Zeke," Pa nodded, a rare smile splitting his beard. He and the commander of Fort Crawford were old friends.

We drew up by the dock and Taylor bent to steady the

craft while Pa stepped out. They shook hands. The rest of us shipped paddles, climbed out, and ran the canoe along the dock onto the beach.

The colonel sighed and shook his head. "Three strapping boys. You're a lucky man, Amos."

"Three's more than enough. You ought to know, Zeke, you have a son."

Colonel Taylor snorted. "And three daughters. Besides, Dick is only five. Time he's half-grown, I'll be too old to take him camping and the like."

"It's terrible," Pa agreed, both of them grinning at the joke. The colonel was no older than Pa, a stocky, broad-faced Kentuckian in the ruddy health of his prime. He had a heavy expressive mouth and bushy dark side-whiskers that showed only a little gray.

"Anyhow," Pa continued, "you shouldn't lack time for it. Seems every time we come to Prairie du Chien, you're loitering about the dock."

It was a joking reference to the colonel's favorite pastime. But we knew it wasn't an idle one. If a man wanted information on any subject that was current along the great Mississippi Valley from here to New Orleans, anything from the state of crops to the state of the Union, the waterfront was the place to pick it up. The steamboat captains, especially, knew just about everything.

Taylor's smile was just a little grim. "It's a rare moment these days, Amos. I guess the news hasn't reached the Blue yet."

"What news?"

"Black Hawk has made good his threat of last fall. He's crossed the Mississippi into Illinois."

"Wow!" said Theron. He hummed a bar of "Hail Columbia." Pa gave him a quiet-down stare and said, "Then it's trouble for sure, Zeke?"

"The biggest trouble this territory has seen since the War of 1812."

We knew the colonel wasn't exaggerating. Until a year ago, few whites had been familiar with the name of Black Hawk, sixty-five-year-old headman of a band of Ioway Sacs whose ancestral homeland was on Rock Island at the mouth of the Rock River in Illinois. Last spring, while he and his warriors were hunting, white settlers had invaded their village, burned their lodges, beaten their women, and plowed up their burial grounds. Before that, whites had brought whisky among them and cheated the befuddled Indians out of horses and furs. So Black Hawk had led his braves on the warpath, destroying settlers' property and livestock, fighting fire with fire. Governor Reynolds of Illinois had sent out a call for militia, but the Sacs had evaded the volunteer troops with cunning ease until midsummer, when it had seemed sensible to arrange a truce.

The upshot of the Rock Island truce council had been that Black Hawk and his band were forced to retire west of the Mississippi and forbidden to recross to their traditional lands without permission from the White Fathers. Seething under what he considered a burden of white injustices, Black Hawk had made camp at the mouth of the Des Moines River, vowing to return in the spring with enough braves "to make corn grow in our fields."

"He crossed at the Yellow Banks below the Rock River," said Colonel Taylor. "Came right across Rock Island hard by his old village of Saukenuk. Of course, the settlers had laid waste to it and there was nothing to stop for. But Fort Armstrong is there too, and the old man showed his contempt for the Army by marching right past the fort."

The colonel sounded miffed. I wondered if it was because twenty years ago, when Zachary Taylor had been a young major and had the job of building Fort Armstrong, Black

Hawk had almost driven him off Rock Island by blasting his troops with cannon borrowed from Black Hawk's British friends. But it appeared that something more was riling Taylor. "The ice was out of the Mississippi by late March this year. Plenty of time for General Atkinson to have moved troops up from St. Louis and fortify Rock Island. He could have stopped Black Hawk cold right there. Instead Atkinson tried to negotiate with the chief of the Sac nation, Keokuk."

"To stop Black Hawk?" Pa raised his brows. "I've heard he and Keokuk aren't on best of terms."

"Exactly. Keokuk wants peace with us. Black Hawk ignored the peace parley and proceeded up the Rock River with his band. He's deep inside Illinois now with five hundred warriors, all their women and children and belongings. He's come to stay, and it will take hundreds of troops to root him out. The U. S. Army can't handle it alone. So Atkinson asked Governor Reynolds to call out the state militia and raise a force of civilian recruits. We're asking for volunteers from Michigan Territory too." Colonel Taylor gave Pa a keen glance. "What about you and your boys, Amos?"

Pa shook his head. "It's no fight of ours."

"You'll find it hard to stand apart. People will say if you're not against the Indians, you're for 'em. A renegade."

"Let 'em." Pa's beard jutted. "I've no quarrel with the Sacs. If they'd been treated fairly, if they hadn't been cheated again and again by bad treaties and whisky-selling traders, if settlers had left 'em alone, there'd be no war brewing."

"Don't 'opine' that way too freely," the colonel cautioned. "People are mighty edgy. No violence has broken yet, but it's bound to unless Black Hawk changes his tune. General Atkinson hopes that a show of force will persuade him to surrender or at least turn back. I've sent out runners to Helena, Mineral Point, Blue Mounds, Dodgeville, and other settlements. Our own garrison will be moved down to Fort Armstrong in a few days. Atkinson is massing his force there."

Pa rubbed his chin. "Doesn't sound like Black Hawk came to fight. Seems all he wants is to reclaim his traditional lands."

"Out of the question. The government won't accept that, neither will the settlers. Why should they? Black Hawk signed a treaty."

"A wrong-headed treaty that was forced on him."

Ben nudged my arm and grinned. Pa was usually a close-mouthed man, but he'd never made a secret of how strongly some of his feelings ran against the common grain. On the Northwest border in the 1830s, hardly anyone ever suggested that Indians had any rights at all. Colonel Taylor's face squinched into bulldog lines, and he looked ready to argue.

His attention was diverted by a young officer coming down the gravel road from the fort. He walked onto the dock and saluted the colonel. "Beg pardon, sir. Thought you'd want to know those deserters have been apprehended."

"Good. All four of them?"

"Yes, sir. Our Winnebago scouts overtook them several miles up the Wisconsin and brought them in."

Taylor gave Pa a dour smile. "Seems our desertion rate always picks up when there's a rumor of war. Amos, this is my new aide, Lieutenant Jefferson Davis."

Lieutenant Davis responded pleasantly to the introductions. He was a handsome, kind of slender fellow, and he carried himself with a jaunty grace. He had a winning way about him, and his handshake was strong. "You're from New England, Mr. Trask?"

"Massachusetts," Pa said. "And you'd be a Southerner by your voice . . . Kentucky?"

"Mississippi. But you have a good ear, sir. I was born in Kentucky, later educated there."

"I see. Have you enjoyed one of our northern winters yet?"

Lieutenant Davis made a wry face. "Four of them. I like to winter warm, but I've been on duty in Michigan since I graduated from West Point in '28." He looked at Colonel Taylor. "Will there be any orders regarding the prisoners, sir?"

"A flogging for all four. Then they'll be branded. On the parade ground, and I want the whole garrison ordered out to watch. Making a strong example of these men will cause any would-be deserters to think twice. I'll give the order myself." Colonel Taylor thrust out his hand. "Goodbye, Amos. Perhaps when the fighting starts, you'll find reason to change your mind."

"Not likely, Zeke."

We got our furs from the boat, hefty hundred-pound packs of sixty hides each that Pa had compressed into bales with a scissors press he'd made of logs and rawhide. We shouldered a pack apiece and tramped up to the bridge that crossed the slough to the island.

"Pa," I ventured to say, "is that what they really do? Flog and brand those fellows?"

"With a cat-o'-nine-tails and red-hot iron. In time of war, those men would be shot."

Theron chuckled and gave me a cuff on the head. "You want to jine up, Rooster? Sounds like a right hearty life."

"I saw many a man flogged at sea," Pa said. "It's harsh punishment, but discipline has to be maintained. If a man knowingly breaks the rules, he knowingly risks the consequences."

It sounded pretty awful, all the same. I vowed then and there I'd never be a soldier or sailor.

We turned up the muddy lane called Water Street toward the stone trading post and warehouse that made up the Astor post. We entered the office where young Hercules Dousman was concluding a trade with a pair of Indians. He looked up as we came in, a quick smile crossing his homely big-nosed face.

"Ah, Mr. Trask. Good to see you again, sir." He and Pa shook hands. "I needn't ask, I know you've brought in the usual quality of furs. Some of the best."

"See for yourself." Pa undid one of the packs and spread the pelts on a counter.

Dousman summed them up with a glance. "Marten, otter, muskrat, all in fine condition. You've come in a little late, but I can give you top prices for these."

"Those are the prime ones." Pa motioned us to spread out the other furs. "The rest are of mixed quality. I'll horsetrade you for them."

"Fine." Dousman's black eyes sparkled. "I'll give you four dollars a pelt for the best. . . ."

While they were dickering, I looked over the trade wares that were stocked for the Indians. Blankets, muskets, knives, looking glasses, copper pots, and iron utensils. All sturdy goods, for John Jacob Astor had made it a firm policy to trade fairly with the Indians. If an article turned out shoddy, the American Fur Company would replace it, whatever the trouble or cost. But what caught my eye was a Kentucky long rifle. It was a masterpiece of the old gunsmith's art, nearly six feet long from its curly maple stock to the slightly flared muzzle. I reached out and ran a hand over the octagonal barrel and brass mountings. Just the touch made my mouth water.

Theron gave Ben a nudge and a wink. "Look there. Hey, Rooster, that is a man-size piece. You couldn't heist it to sight in."

"Go on, Kev," Ben grinned. "Try the feel of it."

I picked the gun carefully off the rack. I was surprised how light it was, despite its size and length. "She's easy as a feather, Ben."

"Time you had a rifle of your own. Why don't you ask Pa?" I gave him a quick look. "Go on," he urged. "Can't do no harm."

"First time he shot that thing off," Ther cackled, "he would fly clean out of sight with a busted shoulder."

"Ah, leave the kid alone, can't you?"

I snugged the crescent butt plate to my shoulder and lined my eye down the open rear sight to the hair-blade front sight. With this piece you could line on a stump two hundred yards away and hit it clean as a whistle. I swung toward the open door, still sighting, wanting to fix on something distant, a tree.

Suddenly the sights blacked. It took me a second to realize that someone had stepped into the doorway. I lowered the rifle quickly. The man stood there filling the doorway and giving me a long stare out of eyes as small and wide-set as a pig's. Then he stepped into the room, light and silent as a panther for all his bulk. The man who followed him was a foot shorter, thin as a whip. Both carried packs of hides on their backs.

Snap was stretched out on the floor, head resting on his paws. The big man took a swipe at him with a moccasined foot. "Get outa my way, you scruffy bag o' fleas—"

Snap sprang up and backed several feet off, hackles bristling, growling in his throat. Pig Eye let his pack drop to the floor and pulled a steel-bladed tomahawk from his belt. "I ain't walking around no fleabag," he announced.

"I think you'd better, mister." Pa had pushed away from the counter and was facing the big man. He spoke softly, but the edge of his voice could have cut butter. "I think you'd better walk right around him."

CHAPTER TWO

Pig Eye wasn't as tall as Pa, but he was even heavier. His thick chest and arms almost burst his dirty linsey shirt, and his legs filled his greasy buckskin breeches like oak trunks. Yet he didn't appear fat. He looked ready to spit as he said: "Don't fool with this child, big man. I'm half bull elk and half wild hoss. I was weaned on painter milk—"

"And you chew up a barrel of cannon balls for breakfast." Pa didn't sound impressed. "I'm not interested in your lineage or your gastronomic customs, mister. Just don't touch that dog."

Pig Eye's face flushed a deeper red than his tangled mat of hair. "If there's one thing I can't abide, it's a smart-mouth bucko with a gizzard full of eddicated airs. I got a mind to show you what-for here 'n' now."

His small companion was sizing Pa up carefully, and the look in his pale eyes said he didn't fancy what he saw. His long black hair and full beard hid nearly all his face except those wicked watchful eyes and his long blade of a nose. He wore a naked Bowie knife shoved through his belt. I had the sudden feeling he could be a lot more dangerous than his giant friend.

"*Mon ami*," he said softly, "maybe this is not the place. Not the time, eh?"

"That's good advice, Valois," said Dousman. "I won't stand for any trouble in here, Henniger. That goes for you too, Mr. Trask."

Still staring at Pa, Pig Eye shoved the tomahawk back in his belt. The sudden movement brought another growl from Snap. "I seen better-looking dogmeat in a Mandan stewpot," Pig Eye said. "Come on, Gar. Let's hunt up one of them St. Looey traders."

"But *M'sieu* Dousman pays the best prices," Valois objected. "And in gold, *mon vieux!*"

"I'll swap my cache for a barrel o' Nongahela rye whisky and a rusty Green River knife 'fore I wait my turn back of this gold-tongued gouger and that mangy mutt o' hisn." Pig Eye picked up his pack and walked to the door. He gave Pa a final stare. "You ever cross my trail again, big man, you better have dry powder under your flint."

I thought so too.

After they had gone out, Pa said, "I never saw those prime specimens before."

"The big one is Sam Henniger. His partner is Gar Valois." Dousman shook his head. "After you leave here, it would be handy to grow another pair of eyes in back of your head."

Pa grunted. "It's not likely I'll see that pair again."

"Popping up just about anywhere is only one of their unpleasant habits. They're known up and down the river as a pair of bad apples. Some claim they never trap an honest pelt. Just rob other men's caches or bilk the Indians with snakehead whisky. I don't set store by loose talk, but I'd as soon not have their business."

Pa glanced at me and the rifle in my hands. "Well, I do appreciate your quick defense of family, boy. But I doubt that thing is very effectual without loading and priming unless you were aiming to swat gnats with it."

His tone was pretty dry, and my ears burned. Theron snickered. I looked at Ben, but he wasn't giving me any help. I cleared my throat. "Uh. Sir. I was wondering if it wasn't time I owned a gun of my own."

"You were, were you? Well, I've been wondering the same. How much for the rifle and its accouterments, Mr. Dousman?"

"The piece has seen some use," Dousman said, "but its former owner—a farmer from whom I accepted it as payment for a debt—kept it in excellent condition, as you can see. It's been converted for percussion, which makes it a bargain at fifteen dollars. I'll throw in a supply of powder, shot, and caps."

"Done," Pa said promptly.

I stood in a daze with my fists squeezed around the rifle's solid reality, unable to quite believe it. I'd learned to shoot with Pa's old flintlock rifle and a couple of trade muskets we kept around the place. But owning a choice rifle of my own had been a burning wish since I was ten. The kind of wish you can't put into words and wouldn't attempt to with a man as generally distant as Pa had always seemed.

Yet he had seen my want and realized how deep it went. Here he was, thrifty Amos Trask, counting out good sweat-earned cash for a boy's dream. It was by far the finest gift I'd ever known.

For more than one reason. I was seeing my father in a whole new light.

* * *

We went along to the post office and picked up a small accumulation of mail that had piled up since our visit last fall, letters from Pa's brother and Mother's brothers and sisters. Then we bought some supplies: yard goods of calico and strouding, powder and bar lead, a box of flints, tea and coffee and salt, and a new copper kettle for Mother.

It was late afternoon when we pushed off from Prairie du Chien and swung west up the Wisconsin again. We'd be paddling upstream most of the way home—forty miles up the Wisconsin and twenty down the Blue—but the *canot du nord* was considerably lighter now. We never packed much food on these trips, just the usual *voyageur's* fare of rice and dried beans and parched corn. The river bottoms abounded with wild fowl, grouse, and snipe as well as geese and ducks, and getting meat was never a problem.

I undertook to bag our supper and put my first shots fairly wide of the mark. Theron laughed and whooped about that, and also gave my pride a gouge by knocking down a duck on the wing with his old Hall Army musket. What made it worse, I knew it had been a lucky shot. Ordinarily Ther couldn't hit a standing bear at forty yards. He had tried it once and got run up a tree, as the bear had cubs nearby.

Directly I commenced to get the feel of my piece, and I bagged a duck and a grouse in quick succession. That shut Ther up.

At sunset we beached on a sandbar by a birch-bordered point, a favorite camping spot. Breezes passing over the point kept the mosquito population tolerably low and made a pleasant *hush-a-hush* through the boughs. We cleaned and spitted the birds and roasted them on a slow-turning green stick till they crackled in their juices. We ate them smoking hot, the meat pulling away sweet and tender from the bones.

Twilight stained the sky and water with a bronze glow while the woods darkened around us. Tired from a half day with the paddles, we boys rolled into our blankets; Ben and Theron were soon snoring. But I lay awake a long time listening to the chorus of frog song and tingling a little to the feel of the new rifle pressing along my arm. Pa's back and shoulders made a broad silhouette against the firelight as he sat with his thoughts, his pipesmoke mingling with the aromatic tang of pine pitch.

My eyes grew heavy, and I drowsed off. Then a hand was gently shaking my shoulder. "Kev." Pa was bending over me and now he straightened up, motioning me to follow him.

We walked onto the point and sat on a moss-crumbled deadfall by the water's edge. The river gurgled below our feet, awash with starglitter. Pa knocked out his pipe on his calloused palm and stared up at the dusting of stars. I wondered if he was remembering, as I was, the only other time we'd sat like this in the night. I'd been six years old and he had pointed out the Bears and the Dippers and the North Star. It seemed a long time ago, yet I remembered every detail.

Finally he spoke. "Well, you've had a chance to try the rifle. I trust it handles to your satisfaction."

"It's fine, sir. Pulls a hair to the left, but I think I have the difference pretty well allowed for."

"Time you took over a weapon of your own." He spoke low and reflectively. "I did a good deal of thinking about that. Ben and Theron are much like me as to guns. They enjoy shooting, but it's not a prime passion. You seem to have an affinity for it . . . do you understand me?"

"I think so. That's why you got me the gun."

"Well, partly. You're a better natural shot than any of us, and you'll shoot rings around us all before long. It's an accomplishment in which a man can and should take pride, as with anything he does well. But it's more than that. Here on the border, a gun is as much a tool as it is a weapon. Understand?"

"Yes, sir."

"You'll have to care for the piece as a woman does for a

baby. Always clean it after shooting. If you've been out in weather, see that it's wiped dry as a bone inside and out, every part. Never couch the balls in buckskin; use linen patches. Measure your powder to the grain and take care not to overcharge. Practice makes perfect, but never waste a shot, make each ball count." He paused. "Shoot only when you're sure of your target and when you're dead sure what it is you're shooting at. When hunting game, never shoot more than you need. If you think you know all this, be sure you never forget it."

I looked up at the wheeling stars. In the darkness and starshine, it was always easy to think how each was a sun like ours, maybe circled by worlds like ours. Millions of them. It made me feel like a speck of dust and, as always, close to all kinds of wonderings about life and death.

"Pa," I heard myself say, "did you ever have to kill a man?"

It came out brash and sudden, though I hadn't meant it to. He answered promptly and quietly, as if the question were expected. "Once . . . on Lake Erie. Our ship grappled onto a British man o' war."

"Was that the big battle?"

"I don't recall any small ones, Kevin. It was the worst one. Hand-to-hand fighting, pistol and cutlass. I know I shot a man point-blank. I saw his face as he fell. There may have been others . . . it was a confusion I can't well remember. Smoke and noise and decks slippery with men's blood." He gazed at the water, rubbing his beard. "Glory. People always couple that word with any mention of war. I've always wondered why. Glory. A man has to fight sometimes, defend his country and his own, but it's nothing to wish for. Don't ever wish for a war, Kev."

"Pa, don't you think we might have to fight? When Black Hawk—"

"I wouldn't think so. Our farm is well north of the Sacs' line of march. If they hold to the Rock River and the adjacent country, we shouldn't be in any danger. On the other hand, nobody can predict what will happen when the shooting starts."

"But if it does," I persisted, "wouldn't you join the militia?"

"No. Not for this fight. There are different kinds of wars. This is one I couldn't support with any conscience. That's not an easy thing to say when you love your country. Right or wrong, you love it. But that doesn't mean you go blindly along with its mistakes. On the contrary, your duty is to fight to correct its errors, not abet them."

"But Black Hawk broke the treaty."

"There've been a lot of treaties. Do you know when we made the first one with the Sacs?"

"No, sir."

"In 1804. Five spokesmen for the Sacs ceded some fifty million acres of land to the government for an annuity of a thousand dollars. You and I are sitting on the northern boundary of that country now—the Wisconsin River. Now mark this. The Indians retained the right to live and hunt on the land so long as it remained part of the public domain. Black Hawk himself later confirmed the treaty, but later still denied that he'd understood its terms. I believe him."

"Why, sir?"

"Well, the treaty is a white man's invention fashioned on white man's terms. The Indian's government and the way his tribal laws are administered is completely different from ours. Black Hawk claimed that the five chiefs acted on their own, representing only a few of the Sac people. But none of it might have come to a head if our settlers hadn't begun pushing onto Black Hawk's Rock Island nine years ago. The Indians protested to white authorities and were ignored. Keokuk and most of his people, convinced that they couldn't stem the white tide, began moving west of the Mississippi. Black Hawk and his band refused to move, but made no preparations for war either. They'd fought for the British in 1812, and I think Black Hawk believed—still believes—that the British in Canada will back him if it comes to a showdown fight."

"Do you think they will, Pa?"

He shook his head. "Black Hawk doesn't understand pale-face politics. The Treaty of Ghent in 1814 ended British interest in our Northwest Territory. England will hardly plunge into a third war with America over a well-occupied region she couldn't wrest away twenty years ago. Certainly not for a few hundred embattled Indians. Of course they've tried to keep their hand in by giving Black Hawk vague half-promises of support, but after last spring he should know better than to take that sort of thing seriously. As you know, the settlers devastated his town and fields, and when he warned them to get out, Governor Reynolds mustered an army of volunteers and went after him. Outnumbered as he was, Black Hawk abandoned his lands and agreed to retire across the Mississippi, where his band proceeded to starve. All the Sacs want is to reclaim the fields that were taken from them by an unjust treaty. Stolen, really. It would be a small price, a very small price, for a powerful America to pay to avoid a senseless war."

I was quiet for a long time. Pa was rarely talkative at all, and we'd surely never talked like this before. I wanted to draw the moment out. Suddenly, though, I felt tongue-tied. Stars glanced on the water and a fish splashed in the darkness. Nothing was ever as simple as it seemed. Black Hawk was right and he was wrong. Did we have a right to any of this country?

I put the question to Pa.

"There's plenty of room for all," he said quietly. "Indian and white. It's a big country, boy. Too big to be stained by blood because of some men's greed. If that happens, it's possible that none of us will escape being embroiled. War is like that. Let's get to our blankets now. We'll be fighting the river again tomorrow, and that's foe aplenty."

CHAPTER THREE

Back on the farm, there was plenty of work to take our minds off an impending war. We settled into the regular spring routine. The corn had to be planted and more land cleared. Pa planned to put in a crop of winter wheat this fall to see how it would fare. So we boys were kept busy clearing the long strip between our fields and the river, felling trees and grubbing out roots and rock. We put in long back-breaking hours that left us too played out to kick up our heels much during our few spare hours. Now and then I managed to get off in the woods with the new rifle. I did some target-shooting and kept my eye out for small game. And, half-seriously, for Indians.

With the few settlers in the region widely scattered up and down the Blue, we received only bare trickles of news, usually from the occasional river traveler. General Atkinson had organized an army of mixed regular and volunteer troops at Fort Armstrong and had sent an expeditionary force under the command of Colonel Zachary Taylor sixty miles up the Rock River in pursuit of the Sacs. Taylor had halted at Dixon's Ferry and set up a headquarters and nerve center for future operations while he awaited Black Hawk's next move.

Meantime, the whole territory between the Mississippi and Lake Michigan was in a panic. Wild rumors had sprung up of the Sacs and Foxes forming alliances with the Sioux, Winnebagoes, Chippewas, and Potawatomis and sweeping across Michigan as far as Detroit, killing, burning, and looting as they went. Hundreds of settlers had already fled to the protection of Fort Winnebago at The Portage, Fort Howard at Green Bay, Fort Dearborn at Chicago, and to Solomon Juneau's post on the Milwaukee River.

Pa took it all with a grain of salt. He patiently questioned each informant, prying some hard facts out of many gaudy fictions. What the kernels of truth totaled up to was this: Black Hawk had sent runners to chiefs of all Northwest tribes, asking for aid in his grand cause. The Winnebagoes had met in council and pledged their friendship for the United States; other tribes had followed suit. When some Potawatomis had threatened to take the warpath, their chief, Shabbona, had sent his loyal braves to spread the alarm to white settlements throughout northern Illinois and southern Michigan. That was what had triggered the panic. The fact was that no hostilities had yet broken; not a shot had been fired.

All the same, I noticed that Pa kept his rifle lashed to the beam of his plow. He hadn't done that since our first two years on the Blue when a few raggedy Indians still roamed the area. We'd missed an occasional pig or chicken, and one night our oxen had been lifted from the stable; we'd had the devil's time replacing them. After settlers had taken to shooting at any red hide on sight, the Indians had cleared out. Only Joe Devil Bear was still around, but he was friendly and harmless.

One late afternoon two weeks after we'd returned from

Prairie du Chien, I slipped away for a little shooting before supper. I struck down a game path through the pine woods south of the farm. Using twigs, leaves, and what-not for target practice, I'd been making considerable progress with the rifle. So far I had bagged a few squirrels for the stewpot, and I was hoping for a chance at better game.

If I didn't find any, just tramping the pines toward sunset suited me. Barred slants of sunlight turned the needle clumps to bunches of gold slivers and made a gold carpet of the smooth needle-drop trail. Curlews and kildeers thickened the quiet with song. Snap trotted ahead, sometimes cutting off to follow up odd spoors, barking up a storm each time he judged he was onto something. I never looked to bag a whole lot when Snap tagged along.

He was off on a side jaunt when I came into a small clearing where several partridges were scratching about by an old windfall. I half-cocked my hammer and crimped a percussion cap on the nipple. I was taking aim when there came a sharp crackling of brush. The flock took wing as I fired, only bringing down a pine cone.

"Blame it all, Snap!" I yelled. "Come out of there!"

The hazel brush parted and Joe Devil Bear's broad face poked out, followed by his stocky body. I stared at him wrathfully, knowing he could move like a ghost when it suited him.

"You spoil paleface shot, eh, Joe? Big joke, eh?"

Joe grinned. He always looked kind of dignified till he gave that yellow-snaggled grin. He wore a mixed-jean clawhammer coat, some cast-off white man's relic, with his buckskin leggings, and a slouch hat topped his clean shoulder-length hair. About twenty-five, he was the son of a French trader and a Sac woman. He'd grown up with his mother's people, but was a little odd in the head, which is why I guess the Sacs turned him out. They regard queer-acting people as big medicine unless the spirits possessing them seem to be bad, in which case they shun them like poison. Joe Devil Bear roamed up and down the river as he pleased, hunting and trapping, occasionally showing up at a settler's for a handout. At other times he'd come and go, and you'd never know he'd been around except for the brace of quail or quarter of venison left by your step.

"*Me-awn-as-shaw-whai,*" he grinned.

"Sure I shoot badly. What do you expect, rousting about scaring off a man's game?"

I pretended to stay mad at him, scowling as I recharged my rifle. Joe's eyes gleamed as he watched me fill the conical measure under my powder horn with black grains and spill them down the barrel. I took a lead ball from my shot pouch, a patch of greased linen from the rifle's brass-lidded patch box, centered the bullet on it, and thrust it down the muzzle with a stroke of my ramrod. Joe Devil Bear patted the long barrel. "Good gun." He looked sadly at his old Hudson Bay trade musket. "Bad gun."

"*Pen-the-kay-thaun,*" I said. I'd picked up a fair smattering of the Sac tongue from many hours spent hiking and fishing with Joe, and I liked to practice it. "*Kea* make *kay-kay-noo.* My mother will feed us."

"*Wa-wun-nit!*" Joe beamed. He rubbed his belly and asked the usual sly hopeful question. "*Sco-ra-wa-bo?*"

"No. No whisky. No rum. We eat."

I whistled up Snap, and we headed back through the woods. Suddenly Joe stopped and stood listening. He knelt, laid his ear briefly to the ground, then looked at me apprehensively. "*Kit-chi-mo-co-maun,*" he said.

"What?"

"Long Knives," he said haltingly. "*Muc-a-mon.* Many Americans."

"No Long Knives here," I protested. "Friends. *Cawn.*" I tapped my chest, then his. "Trasks, Joe, *cawn.*"

"Many Long Knives. Horses. They come now. They look kill Injun. I go."

He turned and went away through the brush like a snake. I frowned and walked on faster. Joe Devil Bear could always detect things way ahead of me, but a lot of white men coming on horses? Not likely. Sometimes a rider or two passed by our place, but not looking for Indians.

Coming to the edge of the woods, I halted. Our log house and outbuildings were set on flat ground close to the river, the pasture and fields rolling off north and east of them. Everything looked to me as usual. Supper smoke wisping from the chimney. Pa, Ben and Theron washing up at the outside bench. Rowena's pink dress twitching through the aspen grove south of the house as she fetched water.

I was halfway across the fields when I saw the line of mounted men coming up the old Indian trail along the bottoms toward the rear of the buildings. War party. The thought stuck in my throat. But red or white?

I broke into a run. "Pa!"

I must have looked pretty silly running flap-armed toward the house, yelling at the top of my voice, Snap yapping at my heels. Pa and the boys turned and stared at me, and Mother stepped out the door, saying, "What in the world?" I ran on past to the corner of the house and pointed. "There!"

They came up beside me and looked. Pa grunted, wiping his hands on the towel. "Neighbors. Marcus Wynant and Rufe Turley . . . and there's Otis Mangrum's boy. I wonder what's up?"

"Wow!" Ther rolled his eyes and pointed. "Looky there! Red Injuns, boy, that what you figured?"

"I did not!"

"Knock 'em all off, Rooster. Ping!"

I felt really foolish. It was now easy to see that the twenty or so riders were white men. They rode up from the bottoms in a straggly line, and old Marcus Wynant in the lead raised his arm to a halt. Most didn't notice the signal or ignored it, and the ones behind rammed their mounts up among the leaders. Some laughing and hooting and a little undertoned cussing followed, and finally they began to dismount. Marcus Wynant strode forward, a short, massively built, white-haired man with eyes like muddy ice. He bowed to Mother, then peeled off his right gauntlet and shook hands with Pa and the rest of us. Mr. Wynant made a little ceremony of most everything he did.

"I hope you and yours are well, Amos."

"Fine, thank you, Marcus. What is all this?"

"The Third Michigan Volunteers." Mr. Wynant paused as if a blare of trumpets were called for. "We are recruiting up and down the river for our company."

"Sounds full of thunder and portent," Pa said. "Anyone'd think there's a war on."

"Man, there is a war! Haven't you heard the latest? Black Hawk attacked two companies of Illinois Militia. Colonel Taylor had sent them out from Dixon's Ferry to reconnoiter the Sac position. The red devils wantonly attacked their camp, killed at least a dozen men, wounded a score of others, and seized a fine booty of baggage wagons and weapons."

Pa's brows sickled upward. "Is that so?"

"Mr. Wynant," Mother put in, "I'm sure you and your men are tired and hungry. I trust you'll break bread with us."

He bowed again. "I thank you, ma'am, but I can hardly impose so large a company on your hospitality. We have supplies of our own and with your permission, Amos, we'll set up night camp here."

"Of course. Tell me some more about this battle, Marcus. . . ."

Ben and Theron and I drifted among the group of men, returning the greetings of those we knew. These were "neighbors," fathers and sons we'd met at different house- and barn-raisings. A few were strangers, I guess rivermen and trappers. Altogether they made a motley-looking crew, wearing mixed buckskin and linsey clothing, armed with rifles and muskets of every description. Most wore knives and tomahawks in their belts, and several sported three or four Bowie knives apiece.

We three joined Cephas Mangrum. He was Ben's age, a tall, lanky fellow with a sharp wild face, full of lively stunts and quick laughter. We all liked Ceph. He and his father, a widower, had a farm some miles downriver.

"Where's your pa, Ceph?" Ben asked.

"Well, Pa's not keen on this war and someone's got to finish the spring planting, but he figured one Mangrum had better uphold the family honor." Ceph grinned. "That's me."

As we stood talking, Rowena came from the aspen grove carrying two buckets of water from a shoulder yoke. She said a pleasant hello to several young men, but refused to let them carry the water. Ena was a tall, strapping girl, but slender and sunny-haired and pretty enough, and too straight-forward to tease her admirers. She'd wear out a pair of shoes at an all-night barn dance, but never let any fellow think he had an edge.

"Hello, Ena," said Cephas. "That's a mighty creditable sunset, isn't it?"

She marched by him without a word and went into the house.

"Whee-oo," Theron laughed. "I knew our sister would favor one man someday. Who'd a thought it'd be an old cottonmouth like Ceph?"

"What happened there, Ceph?" Ben was grinning. "I always figured Ena fancied you a little. One of those unspoken things."

"Oh, it's a sure-fire fact," Ceph said good-naturedly. "You

remember that corn hop at Turley's barn last fall? I bloodied Sobie Martin's nose for the privilege of the first dance with Ena. She heard about it and told me I was a thorough cad and she was completely disgusted. So I kissed her and she walloped me one. Jaw was swollen for a week. Pa thought I'd tangled with a nest of yellowjackets."

Ben shook his head regretfully. "Sounds like she's sweet on you, all right. I was afraid of that. Another single man will shortly bite the dust."

After we'd eaten supper, we joined Ceph and two other young fellows, Buck Tolliver and Bob Yarnell, by their fire. They were cooking up an elegant mess of corndodgers and salt pork, wrapping the mixtures of raw dough and pork chunks around sticks, and scorching them over the flames. Ceph called it an experiment.

"Soon's we get this recruiting done, I hope we head for the Rock River," Yarnell said. "I am purely itching to catch a red hide in my sights."

"Likely you won't have to budge that far, Bob," Ceph observed. "Now the shooting's started, there'll be war parties all over the country, turning up where a body least expects. My pa was out with Colonel Dodge's volunteers five years ago when Red Bird was on the rampage. He says that's how Injuns fight."

Buck Tolliver snorted. "That Winnebago rising in '27 was just a little old whisky skirmish, boy. Red Bird got taken without a ruckus. This here is a *war*."

"That's what I'm saying. Injuns don't fight by rules. We ought to look to protect our own, not go whooping off way to the Rock River. Black Hawk won't squat on his haunches waiting for Colonel Taylor's troops to catch up with him, that's sure. He will move fast and far."

Tolliver swore. "That murdering old varmint. I hear he

tricked them militia with a truce flag and then just slaughtered 'em."

"That what you heard, Buck?" Ceph waved his stick to cool the smoking pone. "I heard a mite differently. Black Hawk sent three braves with a truce flag to Stillman and Bailey, the two captains of those militia companies. Seems one of Stillman's boys took his rifle and just for fun shot one of the truce bearers. Other two got away. Some more Sacs were hanging back aways, and those Illinois lads dusted a couple of them off for good measure. That's when Black Hawk led a charge on the camp. These splendid volunteers just ran like quail, though they had Black Hawk's party outnumbered five to one. Threw away their provisions, guns, everything, so they could run faster."

"Where'd you hear that?" Tolliver demanded.

"My Uncle Jack. He's got a place over on the Pecatonica. He'd gone down to Dixon's Ferry to join up and came back disgusted. Said Black Hawk had decided to surrender and those gun-happy fools blew up the one chance for peace. Colonel Taylor, who'd ordered Stillman and Bailey not to engage the Sacs, was madder'n a switched cat. Uncle Jack says the whole country is laughing the thing up, calling it 'Stillman's Run.'"

Twilight was edging into dusk; cricket song filled the late evening. Four or five men were squatted around each splash of fire, talking, laughing, swearing. Two or three jugs were being circulated. Mr. Wynant's whole crew seemed to be having a high old time, treating what I'd supposed was a serious business like the biggest lark of their lives. From scraps of talk I'd overheard, it appeared that for most of them, the war merely offered a handy excuse. Some were spoiling for excitement, some wanted to get away from their work or their wives, some were just honing to hunt red game, Indians.

Pa and Mr. Wynant were sitting on their heels at a nearby

fire. They'd been conversing earnestly for some time, low-voiced enough that I'd caught little of what was said. But their talk was starting to heat up. Mr. Wynant's face had gotten red, his voice louder.

"I happen to hold with Stephen Decatur's words," he declared harshly. " 'Our country—right or wrong!' "

"I do not quarrel with the sentiment," Pa told him.

"Yet you're saying you won't join battle against the enemies of your country. By heaven, Trask, I'd not have believed it of you."

"Marcus, do you remember the first part of Decatur's toast? He said, 'Our country—in her intercourse with foreign nations, may she always be in the right.' I'm not really sure that Indians are foreign nations at all. Whether, in fact, they aren't the first and truest Americans—"

"Savages, sir! Murdering savages—"

"And quite aside from that, I refuse to take part in what I hold to be an unjust war. If Black Hawk hadn't been pushed by a gang of greedy fools—"

"Trask, that sounds like the talk of a traitor!"

Mr. Wynant got to his feet, almost bristling with anger. Pa stood too, facing him.

"I'm sorry if you think so, Marcus." Pa's voice held a distinct warning. "I've fought for my country and I may fight for it again, according to my conscience and judgment. If any man here doubts it, let him say so."

But his stare remained steadily on Mr. Wynant, and nobody else offered to comment. The hubbub and talk had dwindled off. Mr. Wynant's face was the color of a turkey's wattles, but he had enough sense not to press Pa further. He glared at the men.

"Get your horses and pack up," he ordered. "We'll not camp at this place tonight."

Nobody moved.

"Did you hear me?"

"Smooth your dander, mister," a man drawled. "We are just settled down and are not strong on batting off in the dark."

There was a general rumble of agreement.

"I am captain of this company," Mr. Wynant shouted, "and I expect my orders to be obeyed. Get your horses!"

"Aw, pipe down, Cap'n Wynant," someone else said. A chorus of hooting and laughing followed and then everyone ignored Mr. Wynant, picking up their easy talk again. He stood staring around him, baffled and furious. Then he stamped off into the darkness. Pa gazed at the men a moment, shaking his head a little, and went into the house.

"Blamed old fancy britches," Bob Yarnell grunted. "Declared hisself captain without a by-your-leave, like everyone should hop when he says frog. Though I don't make out that pa of yourn at all. He could be 'lected cap'n if it so suited him. What about you and Ther, Ben? You boys jining up?"

"Not if Pa says not."

"I'd sure like to go along," Theron said, his eyes glinting hotly. "Man, we're at war! Can't Pa see that?"

"You want to scratch the ants in your britches, that's all," Ben said dryly. "Pa has got the say-so, and he's made it clear we all stay to home. I haven't thought my whole way through this thing yet, but I tend to regard that as choicely sensible."

Ceph bit thoughtfully into his dodger. "Well, right or wrong don't matter now. Things are busting wide open, and I reckon a man has got to fight to protect his own. What else can he do?"

Ben deliberated in his heavy-browed way. "Might be he'd do better to stay to home and see to protecting his own instead of tearing off to a wrong-headed war."

Tolliver spat into the fire. "Well, I knowed there was Injun-lovers back East, but I never looked to find even one this far west."

"Cool your bile waters, Buck," Ceph Mangrum said sweetly. "You're not likely to stumble on a whole lot more. Man, these pork pones are really terrible."

CHAPTER FOUR

May melted into June, and there was plenty to keep us all occupied. Pa worried about the crops, for it was the hottest summer in Northwest memory. We scanned the sky each day and wondered if rain would ever come. Scattered news of the war continued to reach us. Mr. Wynant had gone with his company to Peru, Illinois, where General Atkinson was raising another volunteer army with the help of two militia commanders, Henry and Frye. Meantime the main body of Black Hawk's band was on the move up the Rock River, and the war was moving closer to home. Their goal appeared to be the swampy wilderness at Lake Koshkonong in Michigan Territory, where the Rock had its source.

That was far to the east of us, but Sac raiding parties were out everywhere, making swift, ruthless attacks on settlements and isolated farms, then vanishing like smoke. Hundreds of terrified settlers continued to flee to forts and blockhouses; dozens were ambushed and killed en route. The worst single raid was the massacre of fifteen men, women, and children at Indian Creek.

So we kept a sharp lookout as we went about our work. All

of us except Rowena, who acted dreamy and occupied. This was because she'd made up with Cephas Mangrum before Mr. Wynant's company had left. Cephas had always had a nimble way with girls, but it seemed pretty serious with Ena and him, and I supposed she did considerable worrying that he might stop a Sac ball or arrow. I hoped not. I liked Ceph.

On June 15, a patrol of regular soldiers stopped by. They were part of a detached force from Fort Howard at Green Bay, ordered to Fort Winnebago at The Portage, halfway across the territory. Against fears that Winnebago was a prime target on Black Hawk's list, they'd been sent to reinforce its garrison. Mother and Ena served the soldiers cold tea while Pa told the young officer in charge that there'd been no sign of Sacs hereabouts.

"I'd say, in fact, that you've come pretty far out of your way, Lieutenant."

"I don't want to cause you undue concern, Mr. Trask," Lieutenant Baxley said, "but word come to us several days ago that about 150 Sacs had attacked the blockhouse at Apple River."

"That large a force?" Pa asked.

"Close to a third of Black Hawk's fighting strength, we estimate. Fortunately the handful of defenders, mostly women, put up such a spirited resistance that the Sacs were routed. It's said that Black Hawk himself led the attack. And a day later, word came that a war party of thirteen or so jumped a group of farmers by the Pecatonica River southeast of here. They killed five."

Pa's face hardened to alertness. "Would you know the names?"

"Let's see . . . Bull, McIlwin, Searls, Dull, and Spafford. A man named Spencer and a boy, Bennett Million, escaped."

"Dull—would that be John Dull?"

The lieutenant nodded. I felt my skin goose-flesh. John Dull was Ceph Mangrum's Uncle Jack. The Pecatonica was so close, we counted settlers there as neighbors; all those names were familiar. Suddenly it felt as if the war had come to our doorstep.

"But don't worry about those particular Sacs," Lieutenant Baxley added. "Colonel Henry Dodge's rangers, a company of volunteer miners, overtook them and wiped them out to a man." His mouth twisted wryly. "First victory for our side since the fracas began. I hope not the last. It's been like fighting ghosts."

"But you think there'll be more such raids."

"We think that large band might have split into smaller parties after their bad showing at Apple River. Black Hawk's had all his success with small surprise raids. If one of those parties attacked the Pecatonica farmers, there could be one or several more in your area. That's really the purpose of this patrol. To urge settlers on the Blue to pull out, get to the safety of a blockhouse, those that haven't already."

Pa rubbed his beard. "It took six years to build up what we have here. Buildings, livestock, crops. Leave it unprotected, we could lose it all."

"Not to sound presumptuous, sir, but I'd think that the lives of your family count for more. You're in great danger. Fort Hamilton has a secure blockhouse and is not far from here."

"I don't think you understand our family, Lieutenant. We'll defend what's ours, whatever comes."

Baxley looked at each of our faces, then sighed. "I see. I'd heard from folks upriver that you're a stubborn man, Mr. Trask. I hope you don't find cause to regret your decision."

We watched the troops file away down the river-bottom trail, then returned to our work. But Pa saw that it kept us close to the place. Last fall we'd covered the roof of the new barn with thick sheets of bark, but rain and melting snow had leaked through. So we spent the afternoon shingling the roof. It was easy but slow work. Pa and Ben used wooden mallets to drive cleaving frows into bolts of oak, splitting off thin pieces. Theron and I were assigned to the roof; shakes were passed up to us and we nailed them down. It was a good vantage point. We'd drive a nail, then scan the edge of the woods.

Mother had just called that Supper was ready when Joe Devil Bear came trotting across the fields. Joe had a knack for timing his visits for whenever Mother had been baking bread or pies, but for once he wasn't after a handout. He stood a little way off, grinning nervously at us, looking eager to be on his way.

"Is something ailing you, Devil Bear?" Ben asked.

"No stay here," Joe said. "*Me-aw-nith*. Bad place."

Pa flicked sweat from his forehead. "Why do you say that?"

Joe nodded vaguely toward the south. "*A-saw-we-ke*," he said. That didn't need much translation. "Saukies," I said. "Sacs."

"Where?" Pa said. "How many?"

"Close." Joe raised his hands, fingers fanned. "*Ne-couth-woc-qua*."

"Many." I said. "He means many braves."

Joe's grin was gone. "*Ke-we-thay-me*. All come."

"He is going away. He wants us to come with him."

"No." Pa spread his hands, palms down. "We stay. All Trasks stay. Joe go away quick."

"*Po-shi-po-shi-to*," Joe Devil Bear muttered, then swung away at a trot toward the upriver trail. I didn't see much point in mentioning that *po-shi-po-shi-to* meant something like "great fool" or "fool of fools."

Pa lost no time; he had orders for everyone.

Days before, we'd made preparations for whatever might

come, an attack or a short siege. Puncheon boards had been stacked outside each window, two big water casks had been brought into the house, plenty of powder and bar lead had been brought from Prairie du Chien, and we'd spent hours molding bullets. Now Ther and I were ordered to nail the puncheons across the windows, leaving slots between wide enough to aim and fire through, narrow enough to prevent an enemy from forcing his body through. Mother and Rowena hurried back and forth between the spring and the house, fetching water to fill the casks. Pa and Ben hazed the cows from the pasture with Snap's doubtful help, turned all the livestock into the barns and outsheds, and made the doors fast.

I rapped my last board into place and scrubbed a sleeve over my sweaty face, looking at the sky. Big creamy clouds had been building all day, and they looked leaden and heavy-bellied now, driving swiftly out of the west.

"Well," Ther remarked, "praise be for little favors. Looks like we got some wet coming."

"Along with Indians," I said. "A storm ought to give those Sacs some fancy cover."

"Damp their powder too," Ther grunted. "If that old rummy Devil Bear didn't make all those redskins up. Maybe he had some white lightning in his eye."

Mother came from the aspen grove carrying two sloshing buckets on the yoke. As she went past us into the house, we heard Ena scream. Ther and I dopped our hammers, grabbed our rifles, and ran for the grove.

We found Ena standing in the clearing where the spring was, her spilled buckets at her feet. Her face was dead pale, her eyes staring.

"There." She pointed at the south end of the clearing. "An Indian . . . he was there. I saw his face . . . it was painted all white."

"Let's get to the house," Ther said. He quickly filled the buckets and we hurried from the grove, Ena ahead of us. I backed away behind Ther, my rifle trained on the trees. My heart was slugging against my ribs as we reached the house. Pa and Ben came running up, and Ena told what she'd seen.

"That was a scout," Pa said. "Means they're close and by now they probably have us sized for strength. Get inside fast."

Ben was the last inside; he dropped the heavy night bar in place across the door.

The cabin was one large room with a big fireplace at the north wall and another at the south wall. These were built of pole frameworks with sticks interlaced between the poles and chinked with "clay cats" of mud and straw, plastered smoothly over and whitewashed like the walls. Mother's household utensils were ranged around the north fireplace: Dutch oven, potato boiler, dye tub, copper pots, and brass-ware. A heavy table and benches of whipsawed boards centered the room, and the south fireplace was the parlor area, hand-carved armchairs placed around a bearskin hearth rug. Sleeping quarters were in the loft.

Taking our places by the windows, we were able to cover each side. The panes were made of thin-scraped hide, rubbed by fat till they were translucent and set in wood frames that swung inward on rawhide hinges. They were open now, and peering out between the puncheons nailed across mine, I had a good view of the front yard and the fields to the east.

Heavy-textured clouds covered the sky like gray skin. The air felt thick as porridge. The birds and insects were still. Everything out there was too quiet.

Pa had taken the south window facing the grove. The Sacs could work in nearest from that side, the trees hiding them till they were close. Ben was in position at the west window overlooking the river, where a tangled willow growth along the bank lent some cover. Theron's north window looked out on ground that was pretty much open. Mother and Ena sat on the floor with the three spare muskets ready, powder and shot close to hand.

Snap prowled back and forth across the room, his claws clicking in the silence. He sniffed at my elbow and whined. I wondered if he could smell fear. I felt scared enough, a rat of tension gnawing at the wall of my belly. I thought I was steady, but couldn't be sure. A fellow can't tell much about himself when he's just squatting and waiting.

The thickening clouds had thrown a kind of twilight gloom over the land. The wind was coming up. It probed through the room in drafty fingers, chasing the heat. Outside, nothing moved but the grass. We held tense and still. I don't know how many minutes crawled by.

Suddenly Pa's rifle roared down the silence. The howl that followed shivered like ice down my spine. It was a human sound, and other fierce pounding yells echoed it. Pa slid his rifle over to Mother, seized the musket she handed him, thrust it across the sill, and shot again.

The Sacs were shooting too as they rushed the house. Were they all coming at Pa's side? I couldn't tell anything from my position. I sat frozen where I was.

"Ben, stay where you are—watch the bank!"

Pa whipped out the words as he grabbed another musket from Mother. Ben had started to move over by Pa, but sank back at Pa's order. A bullet tore through a puncheon and whacked into a log beside Theron. He came across the room and dropped down by Pa. Both of them fired, seized fresh-loaded weapons from the women, and fired again.

I snapped out of my paralysis and ran at a crouch over to Pa and Theron. I saw the Sacs retreating into the grove, and suddenly they were gone. All was still again. A stink of burned powder hung in the room.

Pa methodically recharged his rifle, saying quietly, "We hit three. They've pulled back and carried the wounded with them. I don't think they'll try to rush us again . . . not for a while."

"What'll they do, Pa?" Ther's loud whisper was a little hoarse.

"Perhaps nothing. Perhaps wait till dark and sneak up. Or they may try for the livestock. Ben, you keep a sharp eye on that riverbank. Kevin, Theron, get back to your windows, watch the barn and sheds. If you see anything move, shoot."

Ther and I returned to our positions. The wind was pressing the meadow grass in sweeping waves. My heart filled my chest like a swelling drumbeat. They wouldn't cross the open from the south to reach the outsheds, I thought; they'd be exposed all the way. Rather they'd circle through the woods and come up on the buildings from the north. Wind tore at some loose shakes on the barn roof and sent several skittering to the ground. A few fat raindrops hit the sill.

Then Ben's rifle made thunder in the room. He snatched a musket from Ena and handed her his own gun for reloading. Pa said without turning his head, "Ben?"

"One, Pa. Just one. He ducked back . . . wait, I see him. There's another way to my left—"

"I see him." Pa shifted his body sideways and fired, his shot merging with Ben's.

"There's three heading for the barn!" Theron yelled. "Watch your side, Rooster!"

I'd been diverted by the shooting behind me. Swinging back to the window, I saw a slim form dart from cover behind a shed and run for the barn doors. I followed him across my sights. As he reached the doors and tugged at the drop bar securing them, I pulled the trigger.

The Sac dropped to the ground, grabbing at his leg. Theron was shooting, yelling at the top of his voice. "Got him—I got one!" He grabbed a fresh musket and shot again.

I leaned against the sill, quivering all over. A roar of gunfire slammed against my ears. I watched the Sac I had shot twist over on his belly, then push up on his hands and one knee. He began to crawl toward the corner of the barn, dragging his wounded leg. He'd been inside easy range, this reckless brave, yet I'd shot low. I'd have time to prime and load again before he was out of sight. But I couldn't move a muscle. I could see this fellow very clearly as he inched along like a crippled worm, and it was as if we were alone for just this minute, he and I, and I couldn't shoot again.

I watched him crawl around the corner and disappear.

"Kev!" Rowena was nudging my arm with a musket. Suddenly my brain was cold again; I could think and move. I took the musket and passed her my rifle.

The shooting ended suddenly. There was swirling smoke, and its biting reek and a silence in which you could hear your heart thundering. Then Pa saying steadily: "Did any of those three get to the barn?"

"I dropped one square," said Theron. "Kev?"

"I got—" The words made a gummy rasp in my throat; I cleared it. "I hit one. He tried to get inside."

"That third one must have got behind the barn," said Ther.

"The doors on that side are barred from within," Pa said. "Now watch sharp. Their shooting at this side was a diversion. I think they've gotten the idea we're ready for anything they try, so they'll settle for running off our stock."

Rain began falling in whispery veils, slanting away on the wind. Rowena murmured, "Here's your rifle, Kev," and I took it from her and laid the musket aside. I kept my eyes toward the barn, my fingers aching with their grip on the rifle. Silver ropes of rain rustled off the eaves.

A sharp sound echoed through the splash of falling water. Like an ax biting into wood. Ax or tomahawk. Thud-pause-thud.

"Pa," Ther said, "I think that damned varmint is chopping through those doors!"

We listened to wood crack and splinter under the regular blows. The chopping stopped. The barn doors we couldn't see groaned as they were swung open. Only one Sac had gotten inside. But one was enough.

"Pa, let me go out!" Ther pleaded. "I can get that—"

"You'll stay where you are," Pa said harshly. "There are a few others out there, remember? You wouldn't make it halfway to the barn."

That red son was raising a real commotion in the barn now. Pretty soon the oxen came lumbering to view past the far corner, driven out by his yells. The milch cows followed. Theron groaned. "If they get 'em into the woods, we'll lose 'em all." And a moment later: "There, I saw him! He was right behind the cows and now he's between two of 'em. Can't get a shot at him here!"

Unable to contain himself any longer, Ther came bounding past me, his face twisted with anger. He flung the bar off the door.

"Theron!" Pa roared.

But Ther was already out the door, musket in hand. And Ben was right on his heels. I reached the doorway as Ben overhauled him about six steps from the house. "Let go of me, you fool!" They scuffled a little, but Ben was stronger; he wrestled Ther back toward the doorway, half-dragging him.

The Sacs in the grove had opened fire.

Theron broke off fighting and lunged for the door. I stepped back to let him through.

Ben, right behind him, was three feet from the door when he staggered like a poleaxed bull. He'd been hit. His mouth flew open, his eyes grew round, and then he fell forward, his shoulders and head crashing across the doorsill.

CHAPTER FIVE

Theron and I each grabbed one of Ben's arms; we dragged him inside. When he was clear of the door, I hauled it shut and dropped the bar in place. For a moment we were all motionless, all eyes on Ben. Pa moved away from his window, saying, "Kev, Ther, get back on watch. Blankets, Ena. Martha, build the fire up." Kneeling by Ben, he turned him carefully on his back. His face looked bloodless, and a big crimson stain was widening across his shirtfront. Mother gave a soft cry and dropped on her knees beside him, lifting his head.

"It was my doing," Theron almost wept. "God, I'm sorry. Ben!"

"Get to Ben's window," Pa said curtly as he tore Ben's shirt open. "Kev, you watch mine."

I crossed to the north window, my legs feeling numb and rubbery. Ther stumbled over to Ben's place and leaned one hand against the window frame, rubbing the other over his eyes. Ena had climbed to the loft, and now she descended the ladder carrying an armful of quilts. She and Mother were mute and white-faced, and Mother said: "Amos, how bad is he?"

"Can't tell yet." Pa glanced at her, then said quietly, "It's bad. Do as I said, Martha. Build up that fire. Get out your cutlery. Tear up something for bandages. I'll have to dig for the ball, then sear the wound."

Ena spread two quilts on the floor, and Pa gently raised Ben and laid him on the thick pallet, straightening his arms and legs. Ben's head rolled loosely, his mouth hung open. A pulse squirmed in his temple; spots of color came and went in his face. He was alive. But would he live long?

I gazed blindly out at the wind-whipped grove. The sky had split open and the rain was coming down in solid sheets, flattening the treetops. Wet powder wouldn't fire, and the Sacs and their guns must be drenched by now. But I didn't think about that till much later.

I began to shake all over. *Ben . . . Ben!*

Pa lighted several candles to relieve the cabin's gloom. Then he told Theron to come and pin Ben's shoulders while Mother gripped his ankles. Ena held a candle so the light would angle along the narrow blade Pa used to probe for the bullet. Ben was half-conscious, twitching and groaning. Pa went inside the wound with great care while Ben shuddered and tried to thrash around. It took all of Ther's weight to hold him down. Pa probed deeper, and a terrible scream escaped from Ben. The sound sliced across my nerves like a broken-tooth saw. Then Ben's straining body went suddenly limp.

After a minute or so, Pa raised his face. It was shining with sweat. He looked at all of us and slowly shook his head. "Can't locate the ball, but it must be close to the lung. Can't risk going in any deeper."

"But close to the lung," Mother whispered. "Amos!"

"I can't take the chance, Martha. Job for a surgeon . . . and he might leave it there to encyst. At least it missed the lung, be thankful for that. Get your big butcher knife and turn the blade in the fire. Hurry. I want to close the wound while he's unconscious."

The hot knife was brought. Pa used it expertly, touch-on-touch cautery. After a few seconds, I couldn't watch any longer. But there was no shutting out the smell and sizzle of flesh, like fat dripping on a hot skillet. I leaned my forehead against the wall and shut my eyes, swallowing convulsively.

Finally it was done. The wound was seared, the bleeding checked. Theron was shaking like an aspen leaf, and Ena got suddenly sick. Pa maneuvered Ben's bunk out of the loft and set it near the north fireplace. The blood-soaked quilts were chucked aside, the bunk spread with clean coverings. Mother washed Ben all over with warm water and Pa lifted him onto the bunk.

"It's all we can do for now." Pa looked at us, his face haggard. "We can expect fever and delirium when he comes out of it. Be ready to hold him down so the wound won't split open."

"If only we had some laudanum," Mother whispered. "He'll be in such pain, Amos."

"I know." He dropped a big hand on her shoulder. "We'll brew up Peruvian barks to cut the fever. It's all we can do."

The same words again. But it was the empty, helpless note in Pa's voice, not his words, that made me realize just how serious Ben's condition was.

Ben and I had always been close. When I'd been small, I had tagged everywhere after Ben. Next to Pa, he had always been my hero, my idol. But where Pa was mostly distant, Ben had always been sunny-natured, with a deep, laughing warmth that made everyone love him. I'd felt closer to Ben than anyone.

A murderous fury grabbed me. I could have taken on the whole Sac nation at that moment. Murdering savages, as Mr.

Wynant had said. All we'd wanted was to be left alone, to stay clear of any fight. . . .

The rain was still bucketing down in fierce gusts. Pa came over and beside me, peering out. "No sign of anything?"

"No, sir."

"I reckon they've withdrawn. The guns will be useless, and they can't fire the buildings, if they had something of that sort in mind. All the same, we'll keep a watch till dawn. And tonight we'll take turns standing guard."

The hours dragged by like overladen oxcarts. I've never stood so long or strained a vigil. The wet, gray twilight crept into darkness, and rain continued to sob on the roof. Ther wanted to go out to check the stock, but Pa said nobody was stirring outside till full dawn. Mother had prepared a beef stew, but we had little appetite for it. Theron was in a bad state; he kept pacing the room, a hot, wild light in his eyes. He didn't say much, but we knew he was laboring under a weight of self-blame. I couldn't think of anything to tell him that would help.

Sometime after midnight, Pa told me to go to bed. I climbed up to the loft on numbed legs and lay down fully dressed. Tired as I was, I couldn't relax. I lay in the dark listening to the rain and saying the prayers I'd neglected lately. I asked God not to let Ben die and I'd do anything, my brain too fuzzy to know exactly what I meant. But just sort of committing myself helped, and pretty soon the numbness flowed out of me and I slept.

It surely wasn't a sound sleep. In my dreams the Sacs charged the house again and again, and finally they broke down the door and swarmed in brandishing scalping knives and tomahawks, an endless stream of howling braves whose bodies were painted red by blood and firelight.

I woke with a start.

The sun was up, pouring through the loft window. My

mouth tasted like I'd been spitting cotton. I got up as quietly as I could and descended the ladder. Ena was curled up asleep in an armchair. Mother was sitting by Ben's bunk, her face lined and fatigued from a sleepless night. No sign of Pa or Ther. Snap was stretched on the hearth. He thumped his tail at me, but didn't lift his head off his paws.

I tiptoed over to the bunk and gazed at Ben. He was awake, but he didn't know me. His face was beaded with sweat, his eyes varnished·by fever. Mother told me that Pa and Theron had gone out to see how the livestock had fared.

"You ought to get some sleep," I said. "I'll watch Ben."

"No. Thank you, Kev, but I couldn't sleep."

"How is he?"

"Restless. The fever has begun." She made a small attempt at a smile. "Why don't you eat something? I've kept the stew warm."

I didn't feel right about being hungry, but I was. The iron pot was simmering on the trammel in the south fireplace. I got a bowl, ladled it full, and wolfed it down, and did the same again. My juices began to pick up and my head felt clearer as I stepped out into the morning. The wet fields looked rich and dark, steaming a little under the early sun. Raindrops jeweled the grass and leaves, mother-of-pearl on fresh emerald. The rain had done the land good. It was a bright, clear morning.

I almost felt better till I got to the barn. Pa and Theron were standing inside. They looked at me as I came into the runway, but didn't say a word. There was no need. I stared at the carcasses of our three spring calves. Each had been killed by a slash across the throat. My breakfast nearly came up on me. It wasn't the butchery; I'd butchered plenty of meat, domestic and wild, for the table. It was the cold wantonness of the thing.

"They killed the pigs too," Pa said. "I guess we didn't see

them get into the sty. And the chicken house looks like a tornado hit it. Every bird's neck was wrung. The oxen and cattle, of course, will grace a Sac feast. Well, let's get busy. We'll save as much of the meat as we can, put up some in preserves, and douse the rest in brine. I'm afraid most of it is spoiled, though."

"Damn those red devils," Ther said softly. "I'd like to send them all to hell on a burning rail."

I went around the side of the barn where the Sac I'd shot had crawled. I didn't know what I expected to find. The rain had washed away any trace of a blood trail. I looked for flattened grass under the eaves where he might have lain awhile, but he must have found the strength to walk away. Or some comrades had carried him. They never left their dead or wounded behind. A leg wound could develop into something bad. Shattered bone could cripple a man. Infected, the wound might kill him. I hoped it would. At least I thought so, but for some reason I couldn't get up too much dander about the idea.

We spent the day butchering the dead animals, disemboweling and cutting up the carcasses, hacking away the meat that might be tainted. It was a long, messy, and tedious job. By the time we'd finished, we were covered to the eyebrows with a stench of slimy fluids. Mother and Ena boiled a lot of the meat for canning; we pickled the rest in a brine heavy enough to float eggs. Pa, Ther and I got our clean clothes, dunked ourselves in the river, and massaged our hides pink with lye soap, then discarded our dirty garments in a kettle where Mother would boil them before scrubbing, same as for delousing.

Supper was a pretty dismal affair. Nobody had anything to say, and with Ben moaning and tossing on his bunk a few yards away, we might as well have been eating sawdust. Abruptly Theron pushed away his plate, got up and went

out the door. Mother and Ena silently cleared the table. Pa
got out his briar and lighted it with a coal from the fireplace,
then just sat staring into the flames while the pipe went cold
in his fingers.

My nerves were crawling like a hill of red ants. Finally I
couldn't stand it any longer. I had to get away from the place
awhile. Nobody paid any attention as I got my rifle and went
outside. Ther was walking by the river, pegging stones at the
water. He'd want to be left alone.

I whistled up Snap and we crossed the fields to the east-
ward flank of woods. I plunged down my favorite path, trying to lose myself in the familiar pleasure of a sunset tramp.
Wind hushed through the pine boughs; a yellow shed of
needles trickled down through hazy sunshafts. Once, as we
passed through a glade, a pair of martens whisked off through
the flowing shadows like dusky-brown ghosts.

A big gray squirrel raced across the path and up a tree.
He crouched on a limb, flirting his plume at me. I started to
raise my rifle, but the barrel froze in its upward sweep, as if
something had seized my wrist. I felt my shirt dampen with
sweat. I couldn't shoot that squirrel and he, beady-eyed and
wise, seemed to know it. I didn't know why I couldn't, only
that it was connected in my mind with wounding that Sac
brave.

Snap had gone sniffing down the trail well ahead of me. I
soon came on him digging furiously in the loam between
some roots. He pulled up his dirt-smeared snout, a chipmunk
squirming in his jaws. "Let him go! Snap!" My voice was
wild. It didn't sound like my own. He dropped the chipmunk, and it shot back down its hole. I was shaking all over,
and it took me a minute to steady myself.

Snap gazed at me puzzledly. He whined and pawed at
my leg. "Heel," I said. Commands were usually wasted on
him, but he slowly followed me as we went on. The pines

thinned away; we passed into a deep copse of oak and beech. This was as far as I usually ranged on a short hike, but I didn't want to return to the worry and gloom at home. Not just yet. Here it felt cool and peaceful, the best time of day in the woods.

A low growl rose from Snap's throat. His ears and tail were erect, and all of a sudden he went tearing off into the brush. I yelled at him. Last time he'd gotten that excited, he had tangled with a skunk and had been unapproachable for a week. I pushed into the brush after him, my head down, flailing the branches aside with my arms.

"Snap, blame you, where—"

A musket shot crashed through the evening stillness. Snap yelped.

I stopped, my heart banging against my ribs. All I could hear was a gurgling of running water. I plowed through the last brush.

"Snap."

He was standing by a little stream, a clear spring-fed rush that winked over colored stones. It was half-hidden by the big fernlike brakes that shrouded the bank. They hid all of Snap too, except for the curled tail quivering above his back. He was rumbling ominously in his throat.

I plunged down the bank to him. "What in the—?"

I stopped in my tracks.

An Indian lay in the deep brakes by the water. He was motionless on his back, his black-pebble eyes glinting up at me full of hatred. One hand was clenched loosely around his musket, the other around his powder horn. Evidently he'd tried to reload after firing at Snap, but had been too weak to manage it. Black powder had spilled over his bare stomach.

His leggings were soaked with blood. And one leg had a strip of rawhide knotted around it for a crude tourniquet. The leg I had shot him in.

CHAPTER SIX

It was a lucky thing that the Sac had discharged his musket. Otherwise he could have shot me while I just stood over him, too surprised to move. I took a step back, swinging my rifle up to bear on him. He expected me to shoot him; I could see it behind the hatred in his eyes.

Taking stock of him now, I had a second surprise. He was about my age, give or take a few months. Which gave me a peculiar feeling. This boy no older than I had gone to war against the enemy. And the enemy was me.

Maybe that's why I didn't shoot; aside from the fact that I couldn't finish off a hurt man as I would a hurt animal.

I stood staring at him for a long time, and he stared back. I'd never seen a wild Indian this close, and he was sure enough the real thing. He wore a muslin breechcloth, deerhide leggings and moccasins. His bare, coppery torso glistened with sweat. The bones of his high-cheekboned and narrow-jawed face stood out like smoothed-off flints under the streaky white warpaint. His scalp was plucked except for a long, coarse lock interbraided with porcupine quills. His lips were set tight with pain; I think I noticed that most of all.

With my first surprise ebbing, I felt a hate that matched his. My fingers grew white-knuckled clenching around the rifle. Right then, thinking of Ben, who might be dying, it was easy to hate. But at the same time I was taking him in and seeing a little more than an Indian I had shot.

Clots of dried blood darkened the flattened grass around his body, which argued that he'd lain here for hours. He'd managed to stagger or crawl this far, maybe just to reach water, and now he was used up. It gave me a funny kind of shock to think that I'd done this to him, and all I had to do now was leave him as he was and probably he'd die. I wasn't sure, of course, any more than I was altogether sure that this was the same enemy I'd wounded in yesterday's rainy murk. But then I wasn't dead certain of anything just now. Except the hatred. And I could see just as much of it in him. At this moment, it made a curious kind of bond between us.

Snap was still growling. I hushed him up, then sidled cautiously close to the Sac and reached for his musket. He tried to hang onto it, but I yanked it away easily. I took a tomahawk and a pair of wicked-looking knives from his belt and chucked all his weapons aside. Then I eased down on my haunches and gazed at him.

"I ought to just leave you," I muttered. "Might be the best thing all around."

His stony eyes flickered faintly, just enough to startle me. Had he understood my words? Maybe I could fetch him a surprise too.

"*Sog-a-nosh?*" I said. "You know the tongue of the English?"

A black fire struck from his eyes. Hard to say which gave him more of a start, being addressed in his own language or realizing that I'd guessed his understanding of mine. But his mouth thinned fine, and he was bound not to give away a thing. I reckoned his English would be firmer than my spotty grasp of Sac. Black Hawk's people had long been known as the "British Band"; English traders had lived among them for years, and they'd cast their lot with the British in the war of 1812. The band still made regular treks to Fort Malden in Canada to trade and fraternize with British officials. This fellow might even have been schooled there.

So I told him in straight English: "Listen boy, I can as easy leave you to die. Or I can help you get well. But in that case you will be my prisoner, and if you try to escape, I will shoot you."

He finally replied. In his own tongue, and briefly.

After sorting out the sense of his words, I nodded. "Yes, I could shoot you right now. Maybe I'm powerfully tempted to. But there's no need, so long as I can be sure you won't go free to fight my people again. *Muc-quach-how-e-wa.* Understand? Behave well and I will keep you alive."

I waited for him to say something, but he wouldn't. Well, he hadn't said no, which I took to be a sort of cross-grained assent; he was simply too proud to say yes.

Now I began to consider exactly how much of a problem I'd committed myself to. Just what could I do with this "prisoner"? Taking him home with me was out of the question. Because of Ben, I couldn't be sure how any of my family would react. Except for Theron. In his present frame of mind, Ther wouldn't hesitate to finish the Sac off, I knew that. So I'd have to keep the whole thing to myself.

Somehow I'd have to smuggle out whatever I'd need to give this fellow proper treatment. Thinking of it made a sour twist in my craw, for it wasn't a case of wanting to. It just seemed the only thing I could do. Call it Christian duty or whatever you like. He was brave and spunky—he'd shown that in the attack—and I really believed it was my bullet that had brought him low.

The daylight was fading. Whatever I did, I'd have to do quickly. I cleared a patch of ground on the bank and scoured up a pile of sticks. Using a handful of rotted punk for tinder, I struck flint and steel till I'd lodged a glowing spark that I coaxed into flame. The Sac watched these preparations in silence. I indicated that I wanted to examine his leg, and he didn't stir a muscle as I tore his legging open with my knife.

The ball had gone into his right thigh above the knee. I washed away blood till the mangled flesh was exposed. He winced when I pressed the big thighbone, by which I guessed that the bullet had fractured it. How badly I couldn't tell, but it wasn't cleanly broken. Feeling carefully around the wound, I located the lead ball under the skin. It must have glanced from the bone and angled backward. A pressure of my fingers caused the bullet to pop free of the wound in a gout of blood.

I heated my knife in the fire while I explained what I was going to do. I figured that being Indian, he'd have the grit to hold still through the cauterizing. He did, except for a few muscular spasms. Pa would have made a smoother job of it, but this had to suffice. When I'd finished, my hands were shaking.

By now the twilight had a mustard-colored glow. It was cooling toward dusk, and the mosquitoes were whining around like small darts. Weather, mosquitoes, and prowling animals meant he'd need a shelter of sorts, in a spot safe from discovery. I thought of the right place at once, and it wasn't far away.

After I'd made my intention clear to him, I hoisted the Sac to his feet, slinging his arm around my neck and supporting him. He didn't argue or struggle, but I didn't consider that this meant he'd accepted captivity. Wounded and helpless, he'd go along with whatever I proposed so long as it suited his purpose, no longer.

We floundered slowly through the darkening woods, he

hobbling on one leg and throwing his full weight on me. He was my size and a hefty burden, and I was sweating and tired when we reached the cave.

It was located at the base of a sudden slope several hundred yards north of where I'd found him. Three summers ago, a storm had uprooted a giant pine, toppling it upslope. I'd been twelve at the time. Coming on the fallen tree and seeing how the splayed root system stuck out from the hillslant like a natural canopy, I'd been taken with the notion of digging a pirate cave underneath. I'd burrowed deep into the hillside, hollowing out a wide, arched tunnel. At about the same time I'd been growing beyond that kind of kid game, and the cave had been abandoned these three years. Brush had grown across its mouth and the roof might be caved in, for all I knew.

I eased the Sac to the ground, parted the brush, and peered into the gloomy hole. I couldn't make out too much, but the roof and walls seemed intact. I poked around inside with a long stick to roust out any snakes or other tenants, but the cave was clean. Half-dragging the Sac through the narrow entrance, I stretched him out on a bed of dry gravel.

"I'll be back tomorrow," I said. "You might crawl away from here whenever you've a mind to, but I wouldn't advise it. Unless you want to die in the woods by yourself."

He didn't consider that worth replying to.

I backed out of the hole and returned to the stream. The dusklight was going fast. After retrieving my rifle and the Sac's weapons, I started for home at a fast trot. On the way, I paused long enough to cache the musket, tomahawk, and knives inside a hollow tree. Whippoorwill sound coasted through the forest; fireflies winked among the trees like green sparks. First darkness had settled as I approached the warm squares of light that marked our house windows. Snap raced ahead of me, barking.

The door opened. Pa stood framed in the fireglow, his rifle in hand. "Kev," I called. He stepped aside to let me come in, a frown on his bearded face.

"You've no business being in the woods after sunset," he said. "You had us worried."

"Sorry, Pa. I lost track of time." In case they'd heard the shot, I added, "All I saw was a lone squirrel, and I missed him clean."

Theron was slumped in a chair by Ben's bunk, his face pinched and sallow. Mother and Ena were still putting up preserves. I went to the bunk and peered at Ben. He was twitching a little in his sleep, and his color was bad. I knew Mother had dosed him all day with medicinal teas to break the fever, but I couldn't see that they'd had any effect.

Theron got up and began to pace slowly, smacking his fist against his palm. Suddenly he halted, facing us all. "I'm going to Rock River to 'list with the volunteers," he said, and looked at Pa. "I'm sorry, sir. I can't just sit by now. I have got to do my part against these dirty savages."

Pa nodded wearily. "If that's your wish, don't worry that I'll try to stop you. I trust, however, that you'll wait until the crisis has passed with your brother."

"Yes, sir," Ther muttered.

Pa sank down on a bench, leaning his elbows on the table and rubbing his hands over his face. "As soon as Ben is well, we'll leave here," he said. "Go to Prairie du Chien and remain there till the hostilities have concluded."

Mother turned around, holding a dripping ladle in her hand. "Amos . . . are you sure you know what you're saying?"

"I'm saying I was wrong. Wrong to stay on here. Wrong to commit all our lives to the defense of a farm. It's only property."

"But we've put so much into this place. I know what it means to you. . . ." Mother's voice trailed half-heartedly.

"A hundred farms aren't worth any of our lives."

Pa's voice was rough with hidden strain. I realized that like Theron, he was crushed by self-blame. Though we'd all backed his decision to stay and defend the place, the decision had been his. It came to me that I'd never seen his confidence in himself so shaken, and this shook me too.

"The Sacs could hit us again," he said more quietly. "That's reason enough to pull out."

"You reckon they'd do that?" Ther asked moodily. "They must have lost a few. . . ."

Pa's fist thumped on the table. "Yes, and do you think they're any different from you? That they won't want revenge the same as you want it? The land will still be here when we return. Anything that's destroyed, we can rebuild. We'll leave for Prairie as soon as Ben is fit."

His tone signaled an end to the discussion.

Later, as I lay in my blankets, staring into the loft darkness, I did some long thinking on the feeling called guilt. Pa's and Theron's. And my own too. The longer I thought, the more misgivings I felt.

Had I done right, deciding to keep the Sac boy alive? If I could save his life and keep him a prisoner, fine. But once he'd recovered, he'd surely try to return to his people. If any whites were to die at his hands, it would be my fault. Mine alone.

Pondering it in the uneasy darkness, I came to the conclusion that I was bound to feel guilty no matter which course I'd decided on—to let an enemy die or to nurse him back to health. And take the chance that when my prisoner felt well enough to attempt escape, he might not find it hard to accomplish; for I couldn't be on hand to watch him all the time.

I'd made a choice between a frying pan and a fire.

CHAPTER SEVEN

Next day, it was late afternoon before I could get away without seeming to be suspiciously in haste. Having finished my chores, I shouldered my rifle and with Snap trotting along, swung off casually toward the woods. During the day I'd taken the opportunity, when nobody was watching, to make up a small pack of food, medicine, a copper pot and pewter cup, and hide it at the edge of the forest. Now I picked it up and hurried straight to the cave.

Pulling away the brush at its mouth, I saw the Sac lying in the dim light, his face tipped toward me. Apparently he hadn't budged since yesterday. I touched his skin and found it hot, but his fever wasn't soaring yet. He was awake, his senses alert. His eyes gleamed as they followed my movements. I untied the linsey cloth I'd wrapped around the supplies, then examined his leg. It was swollen and inflamed around the wound, which had a raw, ugly look.

I took the pot to the stream and fetched back water. After washing the leg clean, I tore the linsey into strips and bandaged the wound. Next I built a small fire outside the cave mouth and brewed up a tea of Peruvian barks, red senic, and salt of tartar. Luckily we had plenty to spare; no danger of Ben running shy of medicine, and what little I'd taken wouldn't be missed.

When I judged the brew had steeped long enough, I filled the cup. "This will taste badly, but it will heal," I said in my best Sac bedside manner. I raised his head and shoulders and held the cup to his lips. He drank it straight down and looked at me, a mocking light in his eyes.

"I have never met another *Muc-a-mon* who could speak our langauge," he said. "Not even as badly as you speak it."

Well, that rocked me back on my heels. He'd hardly said anything in his own tongue till now—and his English was perfect. Trying to get back my composure, I said, "I guess you must have learned mine from a Britisher."

"For many years there was an English trader on Rock Island, Colonel Davenport. All the children of Ma-ka-tai-me-she-kia-kiak sat at his feet and learned the *Sog-a-nosh* tongue."

Which gave gave me another jolt. "Ma-ka-tai-me-she-kia-kiak" was a Sac mouthful that meant "Black Hawk." I said, "You're *his* son?"

"I am To-mah, son of Nas-e-as-kuk, the oldest son of Black Hawk."

He said it with enough proud force to pretty well convince me. Black Hawk's grandson! It left me a little shaken. I had a real prize on my hands—maybe a dangerous prize. Why had he made a point of admitting his kinship with the Sac leader?

"If you are wise," he said, "you will treat me well and let me go."

So that was his reasoning. Black Hawk's anger would fall heaviest on any one who harmed kin of his; contrariwise, one who gave his grandson aid and comfort and then turned him loose stood in a fair way of avoiding future trouble with the

Sacs. At least To-mah wanted me to think so. Which needled a quick suspicion in me that he might be lying after all.

"If you're the son of Black Hawk's son," I said cannily, "how is it that Black Hawk's braves took all their wounded with them, even their dead, and left you?"

"When the bullet hit me, I crawled away. I do not remember, but I must have crawled a long way. When I woke, it was dark, I lay in grass as tall as a man's hips. Then I crawled some more. A long time. Finally I came to where you found me."

That sounded reasonable. He could have crawled a long way in the blind shock of pain. If his companions had searched for him, the beating rain had wiped out his trail. They'd give him up for lost and go on to whatever grim business claimed their next attention.

I decided not to mince any words.

"It was I who shot you," I told him.

"Then you shoot badly."

"You have any idea about slipping away," I said with a touch of heat, "you don't have to doubt I'll shoot again. Just remember, you can't move far or fast with that leg. I'll find you sure."

"Do you track as well as you shoot?"

"You can always find out."

Our gazes locked for a hot stubborn moment. I watched hate surface on his eyes like a black scum. It left no doubt what he'd do if our positions were reversed, which made me madder yet. "My brother got hurt when you attacked us. We're not sure but what he may die. I want you to know that so you can figure what I'll do if you try slipping away on me."

His lip curled. "You should have done it when you found me."

"I'm a white man, not a murdering redskin, that's why you're alive!"

He gave a weak laugh. "White men," he sneered. "We have seen what you do when you have only women and babies to fight. We saw it a year ago when Americans waited till our men left Rock Island to hunt, then came to our village of Saukenuk and burned our lodges and plowed up the bones of our dead. At least those Long Knives were not women like you."

For a time I couldn't think of anything to say. I was strangling on my rage. Finally I said, "All right, think what you like. But you remember what I said."

He didn't seem interested in pursuing the discussion. Again I took the pot to the stream, cleaned it, and filled it with fresh water. Returning, I set the pot close beside him with the food I'd packed.

We eyed each other with stares of equal, measuring hatred. I'd said what I had to say, done all that I could for now. Still seething, I headed home through the long afternoon shadows.

*   *   *

During the next three days, I felt like a man walking a tightrope. I worried about Ben, about my prisoner, about the Sacs coming back. Mainly it was the strain of waiting, but there was a sour dread in my craw that I couldn't put a name to.

Most of all, I fretted about Ben. Day by day he was consumed by fever. At times it would ebb off, only to flare back worse than ever. Pa suspected complications from the attack of bilious fever that Ben had nearly died of when he was ten. It had always come back now and again, putting him on his back with chills and ague for days at a time. As always in summer, no matter that the June heat made the house a

sweatbox, we kept the windows shuttered at nights to hold
out the miasmas that were supposed to carry sickness. Pa
believed that they consisted of animalculae, tiny invisible
bodies that poisoned the blood.

No doctor could have done more for Ben than we, but
nothing—shuttered windows, medicinal teas, cold-water packs
to reduce fever—seemed to do a jot of good. Neither did Ma's
constant vigil by Ben's bed. Her face was gaunt with strain,
dark shadows circled her eyes, yet she refused to take more
than snatches of sleep.

Getting away from the place daily without arousing suspicion was no problem. With our livestock wiped out, Pa
had no objection to my keeping the table supplied with fresh
meat. I quickly got back the feel of shooting, and game
was plentiful this lush, warm summer. I'd always return with
rabbits or quail I'd bagged.

Actually, I spent most of the time at the cave. I went there
each day, never knowing what I'd find. At least I didn't
have to worry about To-mah escaping in his present condition. His fever raged high and low like Ben's, though he
didn't seem nearly as bad off. He'd have rational periods
when, weak as he was, I'd feel his restless eyes boring into
me like black gimlets. I could only guess at his thoughts.
He was quick and clever, and the time could come when he'd
feign weakness to lull me off guard.

But that time was a long way off. He couldn't fake sieges
of burning fever or the discolored bloating of his leg. It
was badly infected, and I wondered if it had gotten fly-
blown. Possibly it should be opened up to drain, but I wasn't
physician enough to make a diagnosis. I kept washing the
wound and spooning teas into him and brooding over whether
I was doing the right thing. We had practically nothing
to say to each other, and that suited me fine.

On the fourth day I went to the cave early in the morning, full of gloom. I'd gotten little sleep, for Ben had made the night terrible with his delirious shoutings. Pa had said that the crisis was near, the fever had to break soon. He'd tried to inject his tone with a hopeful note, but it had a hollow ring. So I was worried sick, and not at all prepared for what I found when I reached the cave.

To-mah was gone.

A fierce anger beat at my brain. All the tensions of the last few days boiled up in me, and for a moment I couldn't think clearly. Then I knelt and inspected the ground. He'd left a plain trail crawling away into the woods, breaking twigs and bruising leaves. The earth was furrowed by his dragging leg.

Following the sign for about a hundred yards, I found To-mah face down in a little glade. His arms were outstretched, his fingers hooked deep into the loam, as though he'd passed out during an agonized effort to pull himself a few inches farther. I bent and rolled him on his back. His body was as loose as a sawdust doll. His leg, swollen like a bladder, was leaking a reddish-yellow fluid. I felt for a heartbeat and found it strong. The anger ran suddenly out of me. Where had he found the strength to make it this far?

Bushes rustled behind me. I turned, swinging up my rifle. Joe Devil Bear stood three yards away, grinning broadly, holding out his palms in a peaceful gesture. I hadn't seen him since the day of the Sac raid.

"You always have to sneak behind a fellow? I thought you'd left the country."

"Leave so many suns." He held up two fingers. "Come back see what happen Trasks."

"That's mighty generous of you," I said sarcastically. "I suppose you've been spying on me the last day or so."

Joe's grin more or less affirmed it.

He shuffled over to To-mah and prodded him with a moccasined foot. "Why you help *A-saw-we-ke?*"

Some of the edge left my nerves. Joe Devil Bear could be a Godsend. But if I wanted to make an ally of him, I'd better tell him the full story. So I did, leaving out nothing. Joe indicated that he was distressed to hear about Ben, also that he opined I was a *po-shi-po-shi-to* for helping the Sac. Only a fool would keep alive an enemy who'd cut his throat first chance. I couldn't deny that I'd thought the same sometimes. But I told him this was the true white man's way and that to honor his white father's memory he should consider helping me.

"Joe, Kevin, *cawn*," I added, laying my hand over my heart, then over his.

Which was a pretty sugary appeal, but by now I was worn fine enough to try anything. He agreed to watch the Sac and tend to his needs when I was absent.

We carried To-mah back to the cave. Stretching him on the ground in front of it, I examined the oozing wound. I wasn't sure whether it was draining properly, enough to carry off the corruption, and neither was Joe. More than ever, I wanted to ask Pa's help. But I didn't feel I could take the chance, things as they were.

Still, I felt a load lighter as I tramped homeward. Joe might be a little addled, but he had no trouble handling things once he knew what was expected of him. To-mah would be safe in his hands. I was nearly to the house before remembering that I'd forgotten to bag some token game. I'd just have to say I hadn't seen anything.

The moment I stepped into the house, I knew what had happened. Knew it before I looked at the blanket-covered form on the bunk. Knew it by Mother's face, Rowena's,

Theron's. And by the way Pa looked as he came slowly to me and laid his big hand on my shoulder.

"Kev." His voice was thick and harsh. "Kev, Ben died an hour ago."

CHAPTER EIGHT

We buried Ben the next morning. It was done very simply.
The spot was on a high knoll overlooking the river. Sun glanced
on the water, and tall grass starred with wild roses and ox-
eyed daisies blew in the wind as we stood with heads bowed.
Pa read the final words. "I am the life and the resurrection,
saith the Lord. Whosoever believeth in me . . ." And it was
done. We filled the grave and placed the simple headboard.

BENJAMIN CLAYMORE TRASK

died June 17, 1832

age 20 years

"Grace crowned all his days"

Rowena, weeping, placed a little bunch of heartsease, and a
wild pansy, by the headboard. Mother whispered, "He would
have chosen this spot, I think. It's lovely here." And we
walked back to the house. My eyes were dry and aching.

I'd done my own crying earlier, where nobody would see it. Grief runs so deep sometimes that a body can't accept it all at once. Part of it stays sort of sealed off, unreachable. Nature's blessing, I reckon. Eventually it all comes out. But it takes time.

None of us had much appetite for the noon meal. Afterward we sat around the table and discussed what to do next, not that much remained to be settled. Pa restated his intention of taking the family to Prairie du Chien; Theron was still set on going off to war. So we sat about in glum silence till someone's cheery whistle drifted up the meadow through the south window.

Ena exclaimed, "That's Cephas!"

She sprang up and hurried outside. We all followed.

It was Cephas Mangrum, all right, riding jauntily up the river trail to the whistled strains of "Skip to My Lou." He was alone, his rifle balanced carelessly on his saddlebow. He halted his horse and slid to the ground, a wide grin splitting his face.

"Howdy, folks! How are you all—"

His grin faded, and I guess he read our expressions pretty well. Ena ran to him, hugged him, and burst into tears. Ceph patted her shoulder and sent us a questioning look. Pa invited him inside, and Mother served him a cup of chilled negus. It sat untouched before Ceph as he listened to Pa talk, and Ceph's expressions was stiff and stunned.

"Ben was a good friend," Ceph said then. "I don't need to tell you how I feel."

He rubbed a hand over his face and the burred-out beard he'd grown since we'd seen him last. His homespuns were ragged and sun-faded; he looked thinner than I remembered, worn to a frazzle.

"If you'll show me where the grave is, I'd like to pay my respects."

"Rest a little first," Pa said quietly. "What brings you home from the wars, Ceph?"

"I'm between enlistments is all." Ceph sipped his drink. "A lot of the volunteers mustered out when their three-week enlistments were up. Found war wasn't the game they thought." He sighed. "It's no game, that's sure."

Pa gave a dour nod. "You've learned that, have you? See any action?"

"Not much. Mostly we stayed encamped and weighed rumors and made patrols. Colonel Taylor sent bunches of us to Fort Deposit, Kellogg's Grove, North Ottawa, Galena, wherever there was word the Sacs had hit. Whenever we'd reached the scene, things were over. Either the Sacs had been driven off or we'd come too late to do any good. But we saw plenty of the results." Ceph shook his head slowly, bitter memory grooving the corners of his mouth. "Anyway, the Army is moving in force against Black Hawk—at last. General Atkinson has taken over personal command of all troops in the field. He came up from Peru to Dixon's Ferry with a fresh army of volunteers, combined it with Taylor's force, and is now moving up the Rock toward Black Hawk's stronghold."

"Stronghold?" said Ther.

"Sort of. A stronghold and striking base. The Sacs have taken refuge in the marshes and wilderness around Lake Koshkonong at the headwaters of the Rock. It's a regular maze. All attempts by scouting missions to locate 'em have turned up nothing. The general hopes that by filling the region with camps and patrols, he can force Black Hawk to go on the defensive and finally push him into the open."

Pa bit his pipestem, nodding. "Yes, I'd guess pouring on the pressure is the only way. A strange time for you to absent yourself from the action, Ceph."

"No, sir, best of times. It will take Atkinson a goodly

while to put the run on Black Hawk. General means to make his headquarters on the Bark River, and I'll swing up that way from here. I should arrive ahead of the Army. Then I'll re-enlist. The campaign might last into fall the way it looks, and this'll be my only chance to see Pa and you folks till it's over. Some of the other fellows are doing the same." Ceph made a wry face. "Lot of 'em just wanted a time away from old Marcus Wynant and his Holy Crusade. That's what he treats this war like. You know, sir, if you were to come along to the new headquarters with me, the Blue River crowd would elect you captain of our outfit before you could bat an eye."

"I thank you for the thought," Pa said curtly. "But my feelings are no different."

"Yes, sir. I just thought maybe after what happened . . ."

"Ben's death changes nothing, unless to leave me more convinced than ever of the stupid folly of this war." Pa jerked a nod at Theron. "No doubt Ther will be happy to accompany you."

Ceph looked at me. "How do you feel about it, Kev?"

"I guess it doesn't matter," I said, "I'm too young in any case."

"Well, you don't need to feel bad about that." Ceph paused deliberately. "Mr. Trask, folks up- and downriver have cleared out for the blockhouses. Isolated like you are, allowing you've womenfolk to see after, I'd make it good sense if you did the same."

Pa nodded. "We'll be pulling stakes for Prairie du Chien early tomorrow."

"Good!" Ceph's tone held obvious relief as he glanced at Ena. "The Sac parties are still raiding this area. One of 'em hit the Libby place yesterday morning . . . just a question of time before they'd come after you again."

"The Libbys?" Pa said sharply.

Ceph nodded soberly. "Andrew Lamar has a farm just west of theirs. He told me the news as I was passing through. Old Martin Libby was like you, decided to hang on where he was. Appears the Sacs caught 'em at breakfast, with the night bar off the door. Wiped out the whole family."

We sat in stunned silence. The Libby farm was only fifteen miles away, which had made them pretty close neighbors. I had danced with Caroline Libby at Turley's hop last fall. She'd been my age, a quiet, pretty girl with corn-yellow hair. Suddenly I felt sick. I got up and walked outside.

I'd had the shakes before, but never this badly. A kind of scarlet mist blurred my eyes. I leaned my hands against the cabin wall till I'd steadied down. I began thinking about my Sac prisoner then. If I'd had him before me right that moment, I don't know what I'd have done.

Finally I got the feeling under control somewhat.

Unwillingly, I budged my mind to the problem raised by Pa's decision to depart for Prairie du Chien tomorrow. Exactly what was I going to do about To-mah?

* * *

That afternoon, as Ceph Mangrum was about to take his leave, Theron announced his intention of accompanying Ceph to the Bark River. He'd be joining up where all the action was, or where it soon promised to be. He could buy a horse somewhere along the way, if Pa would loan him the money. And Pa was more than generous, giving Ther fifty dollars in gold and not voicing a word of disapproval. However he felt about the war himself, he no longer believed he had a right to block Ther's choice. Mother made up a bundle of food for both boys and managed not to cry until they'd swung out of sight along the upriver trail, Ther tramping beside Ceph's horse.

With Theron gone, I felt considerably easier about my next move, which I figured must be to fetch To-mah home to my family. What else could I do? Not leave him with Joe Devil Bear, who was tending him as a favor to me and not because he cared whether the Sac lived or died. I couldn't take the chance of To-mah getting well and returning to his people. Anyhow I looked at it, I'd made him my responsibility.

I got my rifle and headed for the woods.

Reaching the hillside cave, I found Joe Devil Bear squatting outside. I told him about Ben and he only gave a gloomy nod, as if he'd expected it or had maybe read it in my face. He said stonily that the Sac was much worse and would probably die, his tone hinting that this was only just.

I crawled into the burrow. The smell almost gagged me. Joe hadn't exaggerated. To-mah was unconscious, but must have thrashed around till he'd torn the dressings from his leg. It was indescribable.

I slipped back outside and, with Joe's help, hacked down three saplings. We used our knives, trimming two saplings into nine-foot poles, cutting the third into two-foot lengths, and lashing these between the two poles to form a litter. Then we lifted To-mah onto it.

As we tramped into the yard, Pa came out the door. I motioned Joe to set down the litter, and we eased it to the ground. Pa looked at the Sac boy and his bloated leg, then at me. For the next few minutes, I did some fast talking. Meantime Mother and Ena came out and stood listening and staring.

For some minutes after I'd finished my fumbling speech, nobody said anything. And I wasn't at all sure how they'd take it, what to expect.

I should have known my family better. What held them

quiet at first was surprise. Maybe they felt no more enthusiasm for the business than I did, but duty was always plain to a Trask.

"Kev, you and Joe carry the boy inside," Pa said. "Martha—"

"Come along, Ena," Mother said briskly. "We'll make up Ben's bunk."

Deep in fever, the Sac had no idea what was happening. He thrashed around so much that we had to hold him down, and all his delirious babblings came out in straight Sac. Now and again he called for "*Kea*," which I knew meant "Mother." Somehow that shook me. Of course it stood to reason he had a mother, but the fact hadn't really gotten weighed into my considerations before. Because he was Indian?

Yes, I guess that's why. I'd done my duty by the Sac, but with less human feeling than I'd have toward a dog, for whom I'd have done as much.

By now his mother must believe he was dead. She would grieve for him . . . some way. Oddly, that idea had never struck me before either. The Sac woman would grieve. Later, when I asked Joe Devil Bear about it, he told me that the mother's grief would be terrible. She would hack her hair off short and smear her face with black paint. She would fast for six months or longer, living only on water and a little boiled corn.

After inspecting the infected leg, Pa said: "It must be opened up. Now."

He did the job deftly and swiftly and neatly, then kneaded the leg free of evil-smelling fluids. To-mah passed clean out from the pain, but he never let out a sound. Later, while he slept, the leg was left open to drain.

When he woke next day, he was weak but clear-headed. He lay there quietly, looking all of us over. I don't think hot coals could have pried speech out of him at that moment. Maybe it would be as well to just let him think about it awhile. . . .

* * *

Two days later, we departed for Prairie du Chien. By then To-mah was doing well enough to warrant his being moved, and Pa was increasingly concerned about the Sacs making a retaliatory raid on the farm. We loaded the *canot du nord* with what provisions and personal belongings we'd require, hoping that what we had to leave behind would be intact on our return. Joe Devil Bear had been hanging close to the house since we'd brought in the Sac, and when Pa asked him if he wished to accompany us, he agreed right away. Though there were six of us as well as a sizable load, the big craft easily accommodated everything.

Just before we pushed off, To-mah spoke for the first time in these two days. He requested that he be left behind. What he clearly meant was that he preferred to take his chances alone and helpless, and no doubt also he harbored the hope that was our fear: His Sac friends might return at any time. I curtly told him to forget it; he'd remain a prisoner till the hostilities were over.

We thrust the craft against the upriver current, turning for a last look at the place as we passed around a bend. It wasn't much, I suppose, by quality standards—the raw, rough-cut buildings and the uneven fields. Yet it was home to us, a place on which we'd left the marks of pride and work. Would it be here when we returned?

The weather held pleasant as we paddled up the Blue River to its headwaters at Lake Marion. Mother and Rowena wielded paddles right along with us men. We crossed Lake Marion and beached on its north end, where we unloaded the canoe. Pa and Joe and I shouldered the huge craft across a two-mile portage to the Wisconsin, afterward litter-bearing To-mah across and assisting the women as they packed over our plunder. Water-launched again, we swung southeast down the Wisconsin.

I'm pretty sure that no wounded Indian captive ever had it as fine as To-mah did throughout that trip. Mother had begun fussing over the invalid as if he were one of her own. He lay stretched on the comfortable pallet she'd arranged on the canoe's bottom; she was continually brushing gnats and flies away from him. At camp stops, she'd bed him down in a cocoon of blankets and prepare special soups and stews for him.

It must have all left quite an impression on the Sac. He would spend hours just watching her in a quiet, puzzled way. Hadn't I helped him? Of course. And Pa had favored him with a man's brusque attention. I think it was the extra kindnesses of a woman that made the difference.

Finally, at our last camp before reaching Prairie du Chien, To-mah unbent enough to tell me that though his own mother would have done no less for a prisoner, he hadn't expected such treatment from a white woman.

"Why not?" I asked, feeling my hackles lift.

"She must be fighting her *Muc-a-mon* blood very hard."

"Staring at him, I began to shake all over. All I could think of just then was Caroline Libby and her shining yellow hair. I turned abruptly and walked away from him. But To-mah hardly noticed. He continued to watch Mother with curious, wondering eyes.

CHAPTER NINE

We'd had some discussion about the best way of bringing To-mah into Prairie du Chien. With the whole territory up in arms about the Sac rising, having an obvious hostile in our company could stir up a hornet's nest against us. The solution we agreed on was to convert To-mah into a good blanket Injun and pass him off as Joe Devil Bear's nephew. Both would pass for Winnebagoes, hired hands of ours, and To-mah had gotten his wound in a Sac raid on our place, which was surely no lie.

To-mah objected strenuously to the idea, though we explained it was for his own safety. No doubt he saw the sense of it, but felt he was losing considerable face by such a deception. At any rate, Joe and I had to hold him while Pa scrubbed the last traces of paint from his face, trimmed off his long, ornamented scalplock, and replaced his leggings and breechcloth with a shirt and trousers from my possible sack. Once it was done, he seemed to glumly accept the masquerade, but I could feel a restless smoldering under his resignation.

Early on the third day, we reached the joining of the

Wisconsin with the Mississippi and swung a mile upriver to Prairie du Chien. Compared to the bustling spring activity of two months ago, the waterfront seemed oddly deserted now. The whole village drowsed indifferently in the midsummer heat. Most of the troops at Fort Crawford had departed for the war, leaving only a token garrison under the command of Captain Samuel McRee. Otherwise the town's lazy currents of life went along as usual, seemingly untouched by the war skirmishes being waged well to the east.

We settled down for an indefinite stay. Pa dipped into his small hoard of gold to buy the necessary supplies and a pair of good-sized tents for sleeping and shelter. He and Mother found a warm welcome among the fort officers and their wives, for folks with quality schooling and background always gravitated toward each other on the border. These good people invited us to pitch our tents close by their "officers' row" and were generous in helping provide our various needs. Like us, they were accustomed to rough living, for an Army officer assigned to a frontier post could expect little in the way of civilized comfort or refinement. His pay wasn't much to brag on either. His wife was expected to constantly improvise and "make do," and her lot was little better than any settler wife's. She had to milk cows, make butter and cheese, can vegetables and wild fruits, sew and patch, and a hundred more things. Decent quarters were so hard to come by, she might be lucky to have a good tent over her head. That was all the McRees had, but Mrs. McRee, jolly and uncomplaining, said that she and the captain expected to have a cabin up by first frost.

The village sizzled under the July sun and waited on the war news. Dispatch couriers arrived at and departed from the fort with fair regularity, and our Army friends kept us well posted on events in the field.

By mid-July, however, the big news concerned not the

Sac hostiles, but a far worse enemy: Asiatic cholera. It was believed that the epidemic had been brought from the Atlantic seaboard by troops of reinforcements sent from Fortress Monroe in Virginia. General Winfield Scott's nine companies of infantry, arriving at Detroit on July 4, had reported sixty cases of cholera in the ranks. From there, the disease had rapidly spread to Chicago, Green Bay, Fort Winnebago, and finally to Prairie du Chien.

Oddly enough, the plague had barely touched the civilian population here, only four villagers being stricken. But so many soldiers of Fort Crawford's garrison came down sick that Dr. William Beaumont's small hospital couldn't contain them all. Some were moved to the village pesthouse, from which you could hear their awful groanings by day and night. Mother joined some ladies of the fort and the village in doing whatever could be done to help the sufferers, but that was mighty little. To protect themselves and their own, folks wore flannel smallclothes and practiced abstinence from strong liquor. And did a lot of praying.

Plague had also caught up with troops in the field. The whole campaign had almost come to a standstill. Word had it that the War Department was so dissatisfied with General Atkinson's limping conduct of the war that they'd sent General Scott to relieve him of command. But Scott was immobilized at Fort Dearborn, Chicago, with his stricken troops, and meantime the cholera had spread to Atkinson's encampment at the Bark River. His offensive against Black Hawk had practically ground to a halt.

Time was heavy on our hands. I went hunting just about every day with Joe Devil Bear, who seemed to have attached himself to our family on a permanent basis. As we'd been warned against roving parties of renegade Indians in the region, we never went far from the village or stayed out long.

As much as anything, the awesome scenery along the river bluffs occupied my attention. If there's more beautiful country than the upper Mississippi Valley, you'd have to show me. The giant hills rolled away blue-green in the summer haze, and the crumbling crags of gray rock were like ancient battlements. I can't begin to describe the great river itself, a mile-wide sheet of sparkling blue crammed with wilderness islands. Geese and ducks were plentiful in the river sloughs, pigeons and partridges in the upland meadows. Joe and I whiled away our afternoons pleasantly and kept Mother's cookpot well supplied with small game.

Meantime To-mah was improving day by day. As his strength had returned, he'd made himself a sort of crutch from a forked sapling, and using this he could get around fairly well. Each day he made his way slowly through and around the village, I guess satisfying his curiosity about white people. Since he wore my clothes and talked easy English, the villagers paid him no more attention than they would any of their own. The population of Prairie du Chien was just about three-fourths composed of people with one or more Indian ancestors.

What To-Mah thought about it all, I had no idea. He didn't confide in me, and it got so we hardly saw one another except at meals. At first I'd kept a close eye on his wanderings, but was soon convinced from his awkward limp that his fractured leg would be a long time healing up completely. Till it did, he'd be a fool to attempt escape.

Yet one evening, To-mah turned up missing. He failed to appear for supper, which I didn't think too much of at first. Not being bound by clocks, Indians generally ate when they felt like it. Sometimes To-mah didn't eat at all; other times he'd stow away enough to feed his whole tribe for a week of winter. In any case, I decided, I'd better see about him; so after supper I cruised through the village. When I failed to turn up hide or hair of the Sac, I judged it was time to seriously consider that he might have attempted to forsake our company for good.

Fontaine the blacksmith told me that he'd seen To-mah walking north from the village. That had been a couple of hours ago. "Maybe on the Sukisep Trail you find him," Fontaine said. "I'd look there, *m'sieu*."

The Sukisep Trail led from Prairie du Chien up to the Black River. The Indians had broken out its north–south trace centuries ago, for the "Plain of the Dog" had been a trade center of the tribes even before the coming of the French. Whatever To-mah had in mind, I'd have to hurry if I were to overtake him before dark. Already it was drawing past sunset.

I crossed a meadow where goldenrod and purple asters made the sole splashes of color on tawny-dry grass that lay withered by this summer's blasting heat. I plunged into the deep-shadowed beeches and oaks where the trail began, twisting across the high, forested ridges along the Mississippi's east bank. Here and there the river sparkled through breaks in the trees. Swooping nighthawks made tearing sounds in the evening stillness.

I covered ground quickly for a half mile or so, Snap trotting ahead of me. Pretty soon he raced way ahead and turned out of sight, then gave a short, sharp bark. I came around the turn and saw To-mah sitting with his back against a big oak, his good knee drawn up, his bad leg stretched out before him. Snap stood sniffing at him, wagging his tail.

"What do you think you're up to?" I asked.

"I am sitting."

"You can sit just as well back in town."

"Yes, but I cannot get away from the stink of white people there."

Now, it's true an Indian doesn't generally fancy white

smells any better than a white man likes Indian smells, but I knew I was being jeered. Also I figured that he had taken this trek to test his strength. Possibly to try out his leg without the crotched staff too, though it lay beside him now.

"You are altogether too spry, maybe," I said. "We can always tell Captain McRee who you are. I think he would be glad to put Black Hawk's grandson in the guardhouse. Then you wouldn't need that crutch any more."

To-mah's black eyes smoldered. "You would do that?"

"Quicker'n you could bat an eye, before I'd see you get away. Right now I guess if your leg had proved to be mended, you'd be far gone from here."

"It will mend," he muttered.

I decided to let it go at that. "Let's get on back. It's coming dark."

Walking slowly to accommodate his limp, we got back to Prairie du Chien as sunset was changing to twilight, glazing the river with chains of gold. Calls of whooping cranes and swamp owls drifted across the water. As To-mah and I crossed the shore slope toward the fort, I glanced across the slough toward the island. Two men had emerged from the Astor post carrying supplies, which they loaded into a *canot du nord* drawn up on shore.

I halted and took a closer look. Yes, the mountainous fellow was Sam Henniger, the trapper Pa had run afoul of back in May. Beside him, Gar Valois was like a diminutive shadow. Both men saw me, and Henniger grunted something to Valois, who nodded. Then they climbed into the "north canoe" and pushed off.

I had a sudden feeling of uneasiness. I looked at To-mah. "Have you ever seen those men before?"

He shrugged. "All white men look the same to me. Why do you ask?"

"I thought you might know them from some place. It's said those two have had dealings with redmen."

He gave me a shrewd glance. "Maybe *you* have seen these men before, eh?"

I briefly told him of that previous encounter with Henniger and Valois.

"The big one," To-mah said then, "is an enemy of your father?"

"I guess you'd say that."

He nodded his understanding. You don't have to explain grudge-bearing to an Indian. "If something happened to your father," he said thoughtfully, "your mother would be very sad."

A statement of the obvious, it didn't seem to require any comment. But I thought about it a good deal afterward. In his own way, To-mah seemed to have taken an interest in our concerns. Exactly what, I wondered, did that mean to a savage?

* * *

In the days that followed, I kept a closer eye on him. Since I didn't doubt the keeness of To-mah's desire to get the stink of white people permanently out of his nostrils, I gave him a plain warning—which was to stay inside the village at all times unless I was with him. If he tried sneaking off again, I'd tell Captain McRee who he really was and urge him to take whatever safeguards he figured necessary. I wasn't sure the warning really took, nor was I certain whether or not he was feigning the continuing difficulty with his leg. In reality, it might be getting better right along.

So I dropped my daily hunting forays with Joe Devil Bear in favor of sticking close to the Sac. I did not fancy this state of affairs any more than To-mah did, but presently, since we couldn't spend all our time just glowering at each

other, we fell into a kind of cross-grained companionship.
We whiled away long, lazy hours along the Mississippi's backwater sloughs, me wetting a line for fish that prowled deep
spots along the bank. Dangling a line with a baited hook on
it made no sense to To-mah, even after I explained it as a
sport. The only sensible way to catch fish, he said, was to
spear them. He demonstrated by making a spear and using it,
which looked like great fun. But I didn't say so aloud, not
wanting to grant him a tiny edge on me. We were poles
apart, and there didn't seem any point trying to bridge the
gap.

All the same, a bridge was being laid little by little, at
the rate of about one plank a day. It happened with no conscious effort on our parts, as we learned about each other by
grudging degrees. Some of this came out pretty bitterly,
making the bridge a pretty flimsy one at first. I could knock
a plank out of kilter any time just by thinking of Ben or of
Caroline Libby. Still I began to see, as I hadn't from Pa only
telling me, how deep the Sacs' grievances ran.

"When Black Hawk was young," To-mah said, "all the
valley of the Mississippi belonged to the Sac people, from
the mouth of the Wisconsin to the Portage des Sioux at the
mouth of the Missouri. We were rich in goods and game
and crops. In his lifetime, my grandfather has seen it nibbled
away by you whites until very little is left."

"You signed a treaty in 1804," I reminded him, "and
several more after that. You can't deny—"

That, you see, was the big hitch. The point where white
and red views broke into clean separation and heated re-
criminations took over. The Indians had different concepts
of authority and ownership; these pretty much varied from
individual to individual. As a result, many redmen refused
to accept treaties made by men of good will on both sides.
Yet the same was true of some whites, quite aside from all

the treachery and double-dealing that went on in high places. The regular Army, braced by rank and discipline, was usually an effective peace-keeper on the frontier. It was bad eggs among the undisciplined civilians, settlers and miners and land speculators, who'd repeatedly provoked the Indians to bloody warfare.

Not that this kind of thinking came to me all at once. In fact, if Pa's balanced judgment hadn't prepared the soil, I doubt whether any of To-mah's arguments would have seeded themselves. At first I related myself much better to other things he told me. I found that the favorite pastimes of white and Indian boys were basically the same, games and hunting and so on; a lot of things were the same if you poked below the surface a ways. So a sort of reluctant bond grew between us. Not a warm and cozy tie, by any means. When we weren't wrangling, we were usually trying to outbrag each other regarding the respective merits of our people. But we *were* talking.

I still didn't relax my vigilance. To-mah never hinted as much, but I figured it deeply rankled him to be indebted to a family of whites, faring comfortably in the enemy camp while his people were fighting and dying—even starving, according to some stories—for their cause, for their very existence.

Well, let him scratch his itch. He wasn't rejoining his people if I could help it.

CHAPTER TEN

Toward the end of July, the fortunes of war began tipping sharply. Suddenly the campaign, which had promised to stretch into autumn, was drawing toward a swift, bloody close. Pa had been at the fort headquarters visiting with Captain McRee that afternoon—July 23 it was—when a Winnebago runner arrived with a bunch of dispatches. And while we sat at the makeshift table outside our tents and ate supper, Pa told us the news.

Black Hawk was on the run. He had given up the fight.

"It seems," said Pa, "that General Atkinson's Bark River camp was running low on provisions, so he sent a gang of militia headed by General James Henry and Colonel Henry Dodge over to Fort Winnebago to fetch back some more. They ran across a bunch of Winnebagoes who offered to lead 'em to Black Hawk's hidden camp—but one, Little Thunder, had misgivings and went ahead to warn Black Hawk. The Sacs fled toward the Four Lakes region, and Henry and Dodge pursued them. The troops discarded all their baggage and provisions in order to hold the trail."

"Did they overtake them?" asked Rowena.

Pa nodded. "But Black Hawk outwitted them. First he fled northeast, then veered back due west. He'd obviously decided to escape across the Mississippi, but the militia overtook him two days ago on the heights of the Wisconsin. That's about eighty miles east of here. He fought a delaying action—sacrificed some of his men while the rest withdrew onto a big hill with the women and children. There they built up some tall fires, but only to hold the soldiers' attention—a ruse. That night they escaped down a saddle on the hill's west side and got to the Wisconsin River." Pa smiled a little, shaking his head. "You have to get up early to slip one over on that old Sac."

I glanced at To-mah. His eyes gleamed darkly, but he never said a word—just sat and pushed the food on his plate around with the fork he'd learned to use passably. The rest didn't know what I did: that he was Black Hawk's grandson.

"Apparently," Pa went on, "the Sacs worked all night to build rafts, on which they sent the weakest of the women, children, and old people down the Wisconsin. The rest of the band headed overland toward the Mississippi."

"Not toward Prairie du Chien, I hope," said Mother.

"No, they appear to be making for a crosspoint well north of here. They'll hardly want to risk a battle with the garrison at Fort Crawford."

"Well, it's fortunate they can't know what mischief the cholera's wrought. At least half the troops down . . ."

"According to all reports, Martha, the Sacs are far worse off. Henry and Dodge had more than seven hundred men in their combined brigades. A good two hundred were too wasted by sickness to participate in the fight at Wisconsin Heights. Yet Henry reported that they had the Sac braves outnumbered nearly five to one."

To-mah caught up his crutch leaning against the table, swung to his feet, and limped away.

"Poor lad," Mother murmured. "His people and ours . . . and there seems so little sense to any of it. Where do you think it will end . . . when?"

"Mighty soon, I think," Pa said. "Black Hawk is already on the run. Now General Atkinson's reforming his army at Blue Mounds, pulling hundreds of regular and militia troops in from the field. He means to pursue and capture Black Hawk before he reaches the Mississippi."

"Soon," Mother echoed. "Oh, I hope so."

We'd had no word of Theron since he and Ceph Mangrum had departed for the Bark River. But then it wasn't likely we'd hear anything until the war was definitely concluded. So we'd all been feeling the grip of a particular anxiety. . . .

We were still sitting around the table when Joe Devil Bear, who had been missing since yesterday, made his appearance. He came reeling across the compound from the nearby woods, a big, foolish smile on his face. Pretty soon he missed a step and went down heavily on his rear. He just sat there grinning. Pa got up and walked over to him, helping him up.

"You've been drinking, haven't you, Joe?"

"Yaaah," Joe chortled. "Much *zhu-mi-na-ka*. Much."

I said: "*Zhu-mi-na-ka?*"

"Winnebago word for 'firewater,'" Pa snapped. "What I'd like to know, where did our friend encounter Winnebagoes and whisky in conjunction? That's about as lethal a combination as I can think of. Where?" He shook Joe by the shoulder. "Where Joe get whisky?"

"No 'member." Joe waggled his head happily. "No 'member."

That was all we could get out of him. A silly, vacuous look and a chant of "No 'member—no 'member." Finally his chin lolled on his chest, and Pa took him to his half-shelter behind our tents to sleep it off.

"I'll have to report this to Captain McRee," Pa told us. "If something's afoot with Indians and liquor, it should be nipped right away."

I accompanied Pa to the McRee tent.

The captain heard us out, his usually pleasant face grim-jawed. Then he said: "It looks like serious business, Amos. After you and I talked this afternoon, word came of Indians attacking a party of trappers on a keelboat up the Mississippi. And they weren't Sacs. They were all Winnebagoes, all young, all drunk. So drunk that the trappers had no difficulty fighting 'em off. Luckily no one was hurt."

"Any idea where these Winnebagoes came from?" Pa asked.

"I'd guess they were part of Red Crow's band. He's camped about twenty miles upriver. Old Crow is neutral in the war, but his young men have been champing at the bit, and if they got hold of whisky, probably nothing could hold them back. But I can't go on guesswork, Amos; I need proof. Your man might be able to provide it. I'll want to question him when he sobers up."

"Of course."

"Meantime," McRee added, "I think we might place him in the guardhouse for safekeeping."

"Is that necessary? Joe will be safe enough with us, and I'll bring him to you in the morning."

McRee assented. We said good night to the worried captain and returned to our tent.

I doubt there was a white person on the border whose flesh didn't crawl at the mere thought of Indians and strong drink. Feelings againt those who peddled the stuff to redmen ran so high that if caught, they were likely to be hung on the spot. Whisky trading on Indian lands had been prohibited by act of Congress in 1802. It was the responsibility of the U. S. Army to apprehend such traders and bring them before the civil authorities. An 1822 amendment to the law directed Indian agents and military officers to examine the stores of anyone suspected of illicit trade in "ardent spirits." If any were found, all the trader's goods were confiscated, his license canceled, and he had to put up bail bond of sixteen hundred dollars before his appearance in district court. Lots of people felt the penalties weren't half severe enough. Yet they were the only bases on which Captain McRee could move against a whisky peddler.

Unfortunately, it didn't appear that he'd be obtaining information from Joe Devil Bear; for next morning, when Pa went to rouse Joe out of his blankets, he was gone.

* * *

We lost no time reporting the half-breed's disappearance to Captain McRee at garrison headquarters.

"I'm sorry, Sam," Pa told him. "I thought Joe would be dead to the world till morning, anyway. Apparently he slept it off and slipped away before dawn. I suppose he was apprehensive, knowing that white men had seen him full of hooch."

"What's done is done," McRee said curtly. "If and when he returns, I'll want to see him at once."

"Sam, if it was Red Crow's braves who attacked that keelboat, couldn't you question him?"

McRee shrugged. "I doubt he knows anything, and he'd deny it if he did. He has no love for the whites. Oh, he'll be angry at his young men for getting liquored up, but he'll protect their necks." The captain strode up and down his office, hands clasped at his back. "Colonel Taylor had the whisky trade all but wiped out in this part of the territory. By having the Indian lands patrolled constantly, he intercepted all the whisky shipments, located all the hidden distilleries, and had them broken up. But he had a civil warrant to do so."

"Can't you get a warrant?" Pa asked.

McRee shook his head bitterly. "Impossible unless I can

name names, offer the civil magistrate reasonable evidence of a particular party's guilt. But I haven't even a suspicion to go on. If I make a move, any sort of move at all, without that warrant, I, not the peddler, will be brought before a civil court, fined and imprisoned. That's a peculiar provision of the liquor law."

"'Peculiar' is hardly the word," Pa said dryly. "Well, again, I'm sorry about this, Sam. I'll collar Joe for you as soon as he shows himself. . . ."

* * *

Joe never showed himself through the whole humid, sticky day. But something else happened, early that afternoon.

A military transport steamboat had pulled up at the landing in the St. Feriole slough, and Pa and I walked down to look at her. To-mah limped along a few yards behind us. At the dock, we found Captain McRee engaged in conversation with a portly, red-faced man. McRee introduced him as Captain Joseph Throckmorton of the *Warrior*, which was the name painted in black across the boat's white-pine hull. She had a six-pounder mounted on her foredeck, and Throckmorton boasted that the cannon would level half of Black Hawk's mangy band with a single sweep of canister.

Pa cocked an eyebrow. "Do you intend to use that piece against the Sacs?"

"Yes, sir, if they attempt to cross to the western bank of the Mississippi. I was dispatched from St. Louis for that purpose. Of course, we're not sure of Black Hawk's intended crosspoint, but on his present line of march it should be thirty or so miles north of here. The *Warrior* will cruise the river up to fifty miles above Prairie du Chien; it'll take time for the whole band to cross, and we're certain to spot them."

"You seem to enjoy the prospect."

Throckmorton shrugged. "I have my orders."

I glanced at To-mah. His face was unreadable.

Pa dropped a big hand on my shoulder. "Well, boys, how about an hour or so of fishing? Something very simple, very basic. It might clean the taste out of my mouth."

Throckmorton bridled angrily, but Pa turned his back on him and we walked away.

Pa and I got our fishpoles, To-mah his spear, and we hiked downriver toward the junction of the Wisconsin and the Mississippi. The backwater sloughs were dark and pooling under the branches of big, drooping swamp oaks. Close to the banks, they were choked by masses of lily pads studded with lemon-colored blooms. The woods steamed in the heat, sunlight throbbing through the woody canopy above. We gradually separated as we worked down the edge of the river.

I'd picked a nice stretch. I lost track of time, pulling in several panfish and a couple of roughs. When it occurred to me to glance around, I couldn't see either Pa or To-mah.

Then I heard the shot.

As I stood there, uncertain what to do, Pa yelled, "Kevin! Stay where you are."

Heart pounding, I dropped down on my haunches. I heard someone move through the hazel thickets off to my right from where Pa had shouted, and that must be him. I wanted to yell a question at him, but it stuck in my throat.

I heard a rustle of leaves and whirled on my heels. It was To-mah slipping up beside me. Neither of us said anything; we just crouched and waited. Humidity crawled on my flesh. Pretty soon Pa called again, telling us to join him. I ran through the brush to the river's edge where he was down on one knee, examining the bank.

"Somebody shot at me," he said. "His canoe was pulled up here, where the grasses are crushed. Then he pushed off. Gone by the time I got here."

I looked up and down the river. The canoe must have slipped swiftly from sight behind an island. "Did you see him?" I asked.

"Not a glimpse." Pa's face was grim. "I can only guess."

To-mah came limping up and stood gazing at the ground. He bent and touched it, and straightened up. "Big man," he said quietly. "He stood here. Your enemy."

Pa glanced at me, and I said: "I told him about that fellow Henniger. He and the other are still around."

"I've seen them," Pa said curtly. "All right, let's get back. Kev, there's no need for your mother or Ena to hear about this." He paused. "I think you'd better stay close to the village from now on. A man like that never forgets a grudge, however slight. If he got the chance, he might take it out on you or any of the family as soon as he would me."

CHAPTER ELEVEN

We went back to the village, and a little while after that, To-mah disappeared.

I'd gone to the sutler's post just off Fort Crawford's parade ground to purchase some needles for Mother. When I returned, the Sac was missing. None of the family had noticed his departure, and I figured he was trying another sneak-off. Preparatory to finding him, I went to get my rifle. It wasn't by my bedroll where I'd left it. I searched the tent shared by Pa and To-mah and me, went through everything, but the piece was undeniably gone. Vanished with To-mah.

This time he meant business, and he'd made the point clear by taking my rifle. Saying as plain as words that he didn't intend being brought back. It was a warning of sorts, too. At least I took it as such, and for a minute I saw pure red.

When I'd calmed down a bit, I decided that whatever the risk, I was setting out on his trail at once. Alone. It was my job, my responsibility, nobody else's. I appropriated Pa's rifle, powder horn, and shot pouch, then slipped quietly from the tent, nobody watching, and headed swiftly north along the Sukisep Trail.

Snap overtook me at the forest's edge, eager and curly-tailed, but I told him to go back. This was no idle woods jaunt, and I didn't want him getting hurt. "Go on, boy! Go home." He whined and let his tail drop, then turned slowly back.

I trekked steadily for a half hour before stopping to rest. The sweat was pouring off me, for even a brisk walk can tell quickly on a fellow in the thick of wet afternoon heat. I was feeling a little panicky. I should have caught up with him by now, hampered as he was by that leg. Or was he? Before this, I'd worried that he might pretend to be worse off than he was, waiting his chance. Or he could have simply slipped off the trail to baffle me. I wasn't enough of a tracker to read the hard-packed earth.

I could have kicked myself for my carelessness. Probably I'd lost him for good. But I couldn't give up. Not yet. I'd push on as long as I could and still leave a safe margin in which to get back to the village before dark.

I'd started to my feet again when a soft noise reached me. I wouldn't have noticed it except that it stood apart from the normal sounds of a July afternoon, the heavy sawing of crickets, the guttural pumping of a bittern by the river's edge. It was the gentle wash of a paddle being dipped and lifted.

The slope fell off quite steeply to the Mississippi channel below, and there were small breaks in the brush and trees that thickly mantled it. So I just stood and waited for a glimpse of the canoeist. Already I could partly see the dugout through the leaves, gliding upstream, and now it slid briefly into full view.

I had only a momentary look at the fellow in the canoe. But that was enough. It was To-mah!

I could have kicked myself again. It should have occurred that he could easily steal one of the many craft beached by the village, escaping by water with no concern about his leg. He'd merely held off attempting it till he was sure that Black Hawk was heading for a Mississippi crosspoint. To-mah hoped to intercept the Sacs, and no doubt an idea of warning them about Captain Throckmorton's *Warrior* gave a touch of urgency to his intention.

Luckily, coming by the trail, I'd passed him up and even pulled a little ahead. To cut him off, I'd have to get some more distance on him. I broke into a run uptrail, covering about a hundred yards before I saw through the trees where the channel made a bend.

I scrambled down the long slope as quietly as I could, hid-den by the trees. The water was waist-deep by the bank and felt like warm jelly as I slid into it. Hugging the tangles of red willow fronds that hung down to the water's edge, I had pretty good concealment. I waited, resting my back against the bank, holding Pa's rifle ready.

Through the willow leaves I watched the canoe swing into view. When it was just a few yards away, I lunged from cover with the intention of getting the drop on To-mah. But my right foot hooked on a sunken stump. Trying to get my bal-ance, I floundered into a pothole and plunged face down in the water.

When I straightened up, dripping, I was holding a useless weapon, the priming drenched. Worse, when I blinked my eyes clear, I saw that the canoe had pulled over to the bank just a yard away. And To-mah was covering me with my own rifle. I dropped the wet rifle, then wallowed through the muddy water and grabbed the gunwale below the prow.

"Stop," he ordered.

"Go ahead," I said. "Shoot."

He shook his head, his black eyes calmly amused. "Will you make me do that?"

"I'm surely not going to let you run upriver!"

"I am following the enemy of your father. He is a little ahead of us."

I stared at him. "What?"

"He and his blackbeard friend were at the trading post. I saw them. Then I got your gun, and when they left in their canoe, I took this canoe and followed. Not too close, for I did not wish to be seen."

"What do you mean?" I almost shouted.

"You are too loud. I am going to find where they go, then wait my chance to kill the enemy of your father."

I gaped at him.

"I am going to kill the enemy of your father," To-mah repeated very patiently, as if to a child. "This is a blood debt I owe to him and to you and to your mother."

"But you can't—you can't do that!"

"Of course I can. It will be very easy. I will just—"

"But it's *wrong!* Don't you understand?"

"It is the only thing to do," he said in the same patient tone. "Today the enemy shot at your father. Maybe tomorrow he won't miss. Then your mother will cry many long nights. Or don't white women cry?"

"You listen to me!" I gripped the gunwale so tightly my knuckles hurt. "White people don't settle their quarrels like that."

"I'm not white," To-mah said reasonably. "But the big one, the enemy, he's white, what did he try with your father?"

"That's different, he's . . ."

I groped for words. A murderer? But murderers had to be punished. How did you explain the difference by To-mah's lights? An Indian rode a debt exactly as hard as he did a grudge: Both had to be paid in equal coin. Also, his slant on the problem was straightforward and very practical: Get Sam Henniger before he got Pa.

"Look," I said earnestly, "you just can't do it that way.

We have to get evidence on him and then arrest him and bring him to trial. That is how we do such things."

To-mah gave a slightly contemptuous nod. "This I know. So maybe he'll never get arrested and maybe next time he will kill your father. Maybe you want this?"

"No, but—"

"The enemy is getting far ahead of us. Do you want to see where he goes? Then we must hurry."

I decided on a quick compromise. After all, it might be a good idea to know Henniger's whereabouts . . . just in case. "All right, we'll follow. But you won't use that rifle, understand?"

"We will see."

This wasn't getting us anywhere.

I was already gripping the gunwale. All I had to do was keep my arms stiff and sink my weight hard. The dugout rolled sharply sideways and dumped To-mah into the water. He came up spluttering, still clutching my rifle. He couldn't fire wet powder, but he clutched the gun by its long barrel and prepared to swing at me. I dived at him and knocked him over in the water. We wrestled for the rifle.

"Bravo, *mes enfants!* Bravo—"

We stopped fighting and stood as we were, waist-deep in the muddy water, hands locked around the rifle between us. A *canot du nord* had skimmed silently from around the upriver bend, and Sam Henniger sat in the prow, Gar Valois in the stern. Valois was applauding softly, grinning in his beard. Henniger wasn't amused. He laid his paddle down, and when his hands came up, they held a rifle.

"You make too much the noise, my children." Valois waggled a finger at us. "We hear you, we turn back to see. Now you tell us why you follow us, eh?"

"Who's following you?" I asked, bland as butter. "We were just—"

"You're lying," Henniger growled. "I see this Injun kid watching us before we pushed off. Now you both turn up close behind. You best tell us what you're about, and that blamed fast."

"We were just going upriver to fi—hunt," I said. I could have bitten my tongue.

"To fish. Ho ho!" Valois' narrow shoulders shook. "To fish when you have only the gun, that is quite the trick, eh?"

"We're wasting time." Henniger nodded at me. "That one, he's that Trask's boy. I took a shot at his daddy."

"You talk too much, *mon ami!*" Valois snapped.

"Don't worry," Henniger said softly. "They ain't gonna tell nobody."

"You do not mean—"

"Hell's fire, man! Why you think they're following us with that rifle? They are set to make game of me for shooting at Trask. You think I'm gonna take any chance with 'em?"

Valois tugged his beard. "Per'aps you are right. Perhaps not. Maybe they suspect something about us. But it does not matter why. We know they follow us, this one lies about the fishing. *Peste!* You are right, *mon ami*. We cannot let them go."

"I can slit their gizzards right here easy as not. No shooting, nice and quiet."

Henniger looked yellow-eyed pleased at the prospect, but Valois shook his head. "*Par la suite.* Here is too close, why let them be found? It was stupid of you to shoot at Trask so near the village. We will not be stupid again. We will take these two well away from Prairie du Chien. Come, what do you say?"

"All right." Henniger motioned with his rifle. "You kids pull that dugout over to shore and climb in."

"*Non,*" Valois sighed, "*non*. Think, my friend. We must let their craft drift loose. It will be found, and all will think they drowned. The bodies will not be found, but this is of no force. None will blame us, eh?"

"Suppose some 'un knows they followed us?"

"*Vraiment?* Who would they tell? M'sieu Trask would not let them go alone." Valois pulled a pistol from his bright *voyageur* sash. "Pull us now to the bank, *mon ami.*"

He held the pistol on us while Henniger gave a few power-ful swipes of his paddle that propelled the north canoe to shore. At Valois' order, we climbed up to the bank and then seated ourselves between the two.

We started upriver, the two men paddling with strong, easy strokes.

The sun was westering deep. Afternoon shadows coated the water like gaunt fingers. The solid wilderness on both sides seemed to close darkly around the narrow channel we were riding. It was coming suppertime, and we'd be missed shortly. I could picture Pa and Mother's growing worry, their increasing conviction that something had happened. Pa would notice that his rifle was missing. By tomorrow search parties would be combing the woods. Worst suspicions would be confirmed when the dugout was found. Probably nobody had seen To-mah take it; all would assume that we'd both taken it, had met with a mishap, and had drowned.

What else could they think?

Scared? You bet I was. Whatever Valois had in mind for us, I wouldn't have given two coppers for our lives just then. I felt purely hollow-bellied, like someone had scooped me out. But I wasn't so rattled or petrified that I couldn't think, any more than To-mah was. We'd both teethed on wilderness ways and had learned very young what fear was and how to cope with it. You couldn't help being afraid. Thing was never to let it best you.

It was drawing toward dusk when we pulled onto a wide sand bar below a squashed rock-capped hill that was forested lower down. The men ran the canoe alongside the bar; Valois climbed out and motioned us to do likewise. Henniger passed us the supplies that the two had purchased in Prairie du Chien. Then he got out and gave the craft a powerful heave that beached it high on the sandbar.

Henniger went ahead of us onto the wooded bank, walking straight into what seemed a solid wall of foliage. But it wasn't. He bent some branches aside for us and we stepped into a shallow ravine that cut a deep twisting course up the hillside. Trees arched over us like the naved roof of a church, almost shutting out the light. I noticed that To-mah was making it without a crutch, despite his bad limp. His leg was better than he'd been letting on.

The ravine wound upward for about two hundred feet and ended at the entrance of a cave. It drilled deep into the hill, a natural subterranean passage that had been laid bare by the collapse of weathered rock outside. Wild cucumber vines hung in a tangled network over the mouth, hiding it from any but a close observer.

Henniger thrust aside the vines and stepped into the gloomy interior. We waited outside with Valois, who had brought up the rear. I heard steel chunking on flint, and pretty soon a spoon of flame grew on the cave's floor, partly wiping back the shadows. Valois' pistol against my back nudged me forward, and we all moved into the broad-arched tunnel.

I looked around in surprise. The cave had been nicely equipped as living quarters. There was a table and a couple of benches and two wooden cots, all crudely made but substantial. Bundles of fur were piled along one wall, but no traps were in evidence. Henniger lighted some wood laid in a kind of natural fireplace by the entrance, smoke being carried off through a drafty crevice in the arched wall. When he'd built a small fire, he lighted a couple of Betty lamps, rag wicks floating in pans of oil, that were set in niches along the walls. Their smoky light filled the whole back end of the cave. This was occupied by a stack of oak kegs, in front of which stood a large, weird, all-metal device of iron and copper.

Valois smiled at my obvious curiosity. "You wonder about that, eh? We build her ourself. Come look at her, boy. Come, Injun. I show you both."

We went over to where the contraption stood. I followed enough of Valois' explanation to gather that it was an apparatus for distilling raw spirits. Cut the "white lightning" with water, mix in tobacco juice, pepper, tabasco, and the heads of five or six rattlesnakes (to add coloring and "bite"), and you had a quantity of the border concoction variously known as "redeye," "rotgut," and "snakehead."

Cackling, Valois lifted the top off a keg and exposed some of the finished product. "Maybe you like little taste, boy. Eh?"

I shook my head in polite refusal.

Wild horses couldn't have dragged me to touch that stuff. I'd heard too many stories of it poisoning men or driving them out of their heads. Even To-mah, who ordinarily didn't show his feelings, was wearing an expression that told me he shared my feeling and then some.

Actually liquor does the same to a white man as to an Indian, only a little less. Whites built up some resistance to it by swilling it for centuries before they introduced it to the Indians. Ardent spirits never were permitted in our home; I'd never seen Pa take a drink even at partying times, and the rest of us never had reason to acquire the habit.

I looked at the distillery, the kegs, the furs. The picture was only too clear.

"That's right, *mon enfant*," Valois chuckled. "We trade the whisky to *les sauvages* for the furs. Look at them, these pelts, all prime."

"That's more'n I'd say for your whisky," I said. "And if there's any savages about, I don't reckon they have red hides." It was a bold speech, but one that I didn't figure could cost us any more than we were about to lose.

"Shut your face, boy," Henniger growled. "Gar, we best get it over with."

"Patience, patience." Valois laid a finger beside his long nose. "I am thinking. Tonight we have the rendezvous with the Injuns. Suppose these two fall into the hands of these redskins, eh?"

Henniger blinked, then nodded. "I get you."

"Ah, *oui*. This is better than if they jus' disappear, eh? Then people think they drown, but people always will wonder. If people find them kill' by drunk Injuns, so, there can be no doubt. *Voilà*. The Injuns are to blame. You, me, we have done nothing—eh?"

CHAPTER TWELVE

I was put to work loading the *canot du nord* with kegs of the doctored spirits. To-mah was excused from this labor because of his leg. The kegs were plenty heavy, and my muscles popped with the strain of lugging them down the long, steep slope to the canoe. Henniger followed on my heels each trip down and back, rumbling that if I let a keg slip and it busted open, he'd shoot me like a dog.

I gathered from remarks dropped by Valois and him that this was only the second batch of border tonic they'd recently prepared for the Indian trade. It took a while to cook up a suitable quantity with their primitive apparatus. They'd finished making this batch only today, their next rendezvous with Red Crow's thirsty tribesmen being set for tonight. So we'd picked a bad time to get caught. The worst. I didn't look for a quick end at Indian hands.

Still, Valois' notion of turning us over to the Winnebagoes did buy us a little extra time. What good it might do remained to be seen, and I didn't exactly feel hopeful. I had no idea what To-mah's thoughts were, but I reckon they were the same as mine. If we did as told, we'd live a little longer and some thin chance of escape might offer itself.

With eight kegs loaded amidships we got into the craft; Henniger pushed off. We occupied the same positions as before, Henniger in the prow, Valois in the stern, To-mah and I wedged between the kegs in the middle. The two men paddled steadily upriver. Dusk waned into full dark. The moon fanned a rippling path of chainsilver across the open river, turning the scene bright as day. A wind came up and roughed the water; it was out of the north and had a keen edge that reminded me the summer was two-thirds over.

Strangely, that hit me like a blow. Would I see another summer? I choked up a little then, but didn't let go. I was bred tough, I was a Trask; I held onto that knowledge.

I was mortally scared, though, and didn't even try to deny it or excuse it.

My thoughts teetered desperately back and forth, pondering ways out. Both men were occupied with paddling, their guns laid aside. If the *canot du nord* had been an ordinary canoe, it would have been no great trick to simply tip my body across the gunwale and overturn us. But my weight wasn't sufficient to tilt this immense craft an inch, much less capsize it. Another possibility was to dive overboard and strike underwater for shore before they knew what was happening. But To-mah, handicapped by his leg, couldn't follow me.

I thought too about To-mah's self-appointed mission to head off more attempts on my father's life by shooting his enemy. It was a barbarous idea if you looked at it that way, but his intention had been unselfish enough. My interference had spoiled it and landed us in a pretty kettle of fish. Thinking of how things balanced out, I knew that no matter what, I couldn't desert To-mah. I had to stick with him and share his fate, unless a bigger fate showed us some way out of this jam. . . .

We moved quietly upriver for an hour or so. Henniger and Valois veered the *canot du nord* toward shore. In the moonlight I could make out four large dugout canoes pulled up on a limestone ledge. As we beached our own craft, a half-dozen shadowy forms came silently from the surrounding brush and pulled around us in a loose circle. The moon made steely glints on their weapons.

"Easy, my friends," Valois told them softly. "Ver' easy now, eh? Where is Gray Fox?"

The biggest Indian motioned us to walk ahead of him. We were herded up a wide path that penetrated far into the woods. Moonlight picked out our way pretty well, but the ground was so stony and uneven that I had to lend To-mah a supporting arm.

We'd gone about a half mile when red glimmers of light showed through the trees ahead. Soon we came into a broad clearing with a big fire build up in the middle. The flamelight danced in weird highlights across a dozen or so more Indians who were sitting or standing about.

The more that red men get mixed up with white ways, wearing white man's clothing and hair styles and so on, the harder it becomes to identify an Indian's tribe merely by his appearance. Each tribe's moccasin is styled differently, which is the surest way of telling them apart. But at the moment, I could only guess that these fellows were Winnebagoes.

Valois raised his hand. "Ho, Gray Fox!"

A gaunt, youngish Indian rose off his haunches and came forward. "You have *zhu-mi-na-ka?*" he asked.

"Of course, my friend. Tell your *compagnie* to bring it up."

At a word from Gray Fox, about half of the Winnebagoes hurried past us down the path.

"We bring these two," Valois said as he pushed To-mah and me into the firelight. "They spy on us. They know about us. They are big danger, eh? You comprehend?"

Gray Fox walked slowly up to To-mah, grabbed him by the shoulders, and stared into his face. "Saukie!" he exclaimed. "Haaah!" He gave another order. Immediately the braves closed around To-mah and me, seized us, and threw us to the ground. Rawhide thongs were produced, and we were both tied hand and foot.

Valois smiled. "That is ver' good, my friend. But these two must not live to carry stories." He whisked a forefinger across his throat. "You comprehend?"

Gray Fox replied briefly in his own tongue, at which Valois gave a satisfied nod.

"Tell him to trot out them furs," growled Henniger. "We want to load up and clear out o' here before these redskins start dipping into that firewater."

Gray Fox's reply was short and curt. Valois gave Henniger a sly grin. "He says for the man with a pig face—that is you—to shut up. When he sees the *zhu-mi-na-ka*, then we get furs."

The Indians who had gone to the landing were now filing back into the clearing, carrying the eight kegs. They set these down near the fire. Gray Fox pulled a tomahawk from his belt and smashed in the top of a keg. He dipped his finger and sampled the contents. Afterward he gave another order. Three Indians loped into the woods and shortly returned. Each carried a bulky pack of pelts, which he threw down in front of the white men. Valois ran a quick eye over the furs; he nodded.

"Eh, *bien*. The bargain is made. Now, Gray Fox, in three suns—" he held up three fingers "—we will see you at the same place, eh?"

Gray Fox grunted assent. He watched his followers beat in

the tops of the kegs. Valois came over to the fire where we lay bound and helpless.

"Ho!" He grinned down at us. "Do not worry, *mes enfants*. It will be over quick. Get the Indian drunk, he does things quick. Is it not so, Saukie?" He nudged To-mah with his foot. "Gray Fox is only a headman. He is ver' jealous of Red Crow's power. We strike the bargain with Gray Fox. Whisky, the white man's devil medicine, brings many of Red Crow's young men over to the Fox. It gives them the belly to defy Red Crow. Fox's following grows. Everyone is satisfied, *n'est-ce pas?*"

Valois barked a harsh laugh, then hoisted a bundle of furs to his back. Henniger effortlessly balanced the two remaining packs on his shoulders, and the two of them tramped out of the clearing and down the path without looking back.

The renegades were already getting their teeth into the occasion, plunging vessels of pewter, clay, half-gourds, anything that would serve, into the opened kegs of redeye. It was alarming to watch a swift change spread over them as they quaffed the stuff. In no time at all, it seemed, they were whooping it up, getting loud and fever-eyed.

Suddenly some of them laid hands on To-mah and me and swung us up from the ground. Right then I thought our time had come, but they only wanted to chuck us out of the way for now. They dropped us at the edge of the clearing, then commenced a shuffling dance around the kegs and the fire. They whooped and sang, their mood growing more inflamed by the minute. It was a wierd scene all around, the fire gusted to yellow tatters by the dipping wind that thrashed and bent the treetops, the men leaping and prancing and weaving in the fitful light.

"There's a pretty to-do," I muttered. "All you Indians need is a swig or two of bad whisky and you go off like Fourth of July fireworks."

"Yes!" To-mah's eyes swung on me like the black-holed muzzles of a shotgun. "And who makes the devil juice? Red men or white?"

"I don't see anybody forcing you people to drink it." I was suddenly pushed to the defensive and would have dropped the subject, but my idle remark had fired To-mah up as nothing else had since we'd met.

"You make it, but we have no stomach for it." His voice hissed with anger. "You make it and use it on us as you would use guns."

"Now you wait—"

"Then when you steal our land, it is all right. Another drunken redman has signed another bad treaty that takes all and gives nothing. Signed away his people's pride for a headache and a bad belly."

"I don't make the stuff," I snapped. "I don't make it nor drink it nor sell it to redmen, and neither does my family."

"And mine does none of these," he retorted heatedly. "Black Hawk hates your whisky men. Of all your people who have robbed and cheated our people, he hates only the whisky men. Do you think that all redmen are like these?" He swept a contemptuous nod at the renegades. "This Gray Fox, he has to give these fools of his firewater on the sly because if Red Crow and the other headmen of his band knew of it, they would drive him out."

Gray Fox stood on the sideline, just watching, his face like brown stone. I reckon that as middleman with the whisky peddlers, he was savoring the power that the devil juice gave him.

He'd rendezvous with Henniger and Valois in three days . . . which could only mean that another bargain would be struck at the expense of his drink-addled followers. Hard to believe that these braves would swap more stores of hard-trapped prime furs for a few kegs of swill that no hog would touch, but I'm told that once people acquire a taste for it, they will sell their souls to get more. If Gray Fox could fire enough heads with whisky and inspire them to more raids on the whites, he would win considerable prestige with the hothead faction of the Winnebago people. I guessed that that was his ultimate aim.

Right now, he too was being infected by the general mood. He swallowed a large draft from one of the kegs, then joined his capering fellows. Somebody had brought out a skin drum and was thumping it with a fierce, swelling tempo. Every now and then a brave would drop out to dip up a little more fuel, then rejoin the dance. They were working up to a blind frenzy where they might even turn on each other. And then—I had no doubt at all—To-mah and I were done for.

I tested my ropes. They'd been pulled so tight around my wrists and ankles that all feeling had left my fingers and toes. But my sharp tugs brought a bite of pain that decided me to give up.

Something made a rustling sound behind us.

I took a quick look over my shoulder and almost gave a grunt of surprise. Not four feet behind us, flat on his belly under the brush, lay Joe Devil Bear. He held a finger to his lips, warning me to be still.

CHAPTER THIRTEEN

Joe would never make mention of what he'd been doing so near the renegades' whisky camp, and I'd never ask. I judged it would be gross ingratitude to put such a question to him. Besides, I guess it was pretty clear. He'd been drunk when we'd last seen him, and he must have fallen in with this same bunch before then. He'd shown up at tonight's rendezvous too, but had spotted us as prisoners before he'd entered the camp.

At the moment I didn't trouble to sort things out this handily. All I felt was a welling surge of hope, figuring Joe meant to help us escape. I was right.

For a moment he lay flat and still under the hazel brush, his black eyes warning us to silence. To-mah and I had been dumped at the clearing's edge, where shadows lay thick under the trees. This as much as the heavy brush had concealed Joe Devil Bear while he'd crawled up back of us. A few feet more and he could slice our ropes with the Bowie knife that now gleamed in one hand. But the firelight picked us out plainly. Even if Joe could cut us free and remain unseen, what chance did we have of getting away without being spotted?

I didn't look at Joe again. I kept my eyes front and waited. Soon I felt his touch on my ropes, cold steel against my wrist, then a sawing pressure. Suddenly my hands were free. I didn't glance at To-mah, but his faint movements told me his hands were loose too.

I listened to the small rustlings as Joe backed away. Now it was up to us. We stayed as we were, watching the circling braves as they pranced and bent. Half were staggering by now, and the rest of them were getting sluggish. I fought an impulse to roll away under the brush. Move too suddenly and we'd be seen. Wait a minute too long and we'd never make it. Soon they'd be falling-down drunk, but they'd have our throats slit before then.

The crumbling fire threw less light now, and the shadows seemed deeper around us. Along with the men's decaying alertness, it offered what should be the best chance we'd have. Nobody was looking our way. *Now* . . .

Lying on my side, I jackknifed my bound legs, dug in my fingers, and inched by slow and painstaking degrees into and under the brush where Joe Devil Bear was. To-mah followed. Strain saw-edged my nerves, but I didn't dare move faster.

Then a bank of light-filtered leaves lay between us and the clearing and Joe was close beside me, his knife parting my ankle ropes. He silently pointed, and I crawled on my belly in the direction indicated. To-mah came slithering behind me, and then Joe.

When I judged we were deep enough in the trees, I got to my feet. The wind cut like ice against my sweating face and body. To-mah stood up beside me and whispered, "You are clumsy." Joe tapped my arm and motioned, and we followed his dark form through the forest.

I tried to move as quietly as my two companions, but

branches scraped at my clothes, and every twig I stepped on seemed to snap like a pistol shot. Fortunately the drum was still thumping, the braves whooping, wind sliding like fury through the treetops—it all covered any sound I made, and soon even the fireshot gleams from the clearing fell behind us. Then we were on the path, hurrying toward the riverbank.

Water glimmered ahead.

We reached the limestone shelf, and Joe Devil Bear seized hold of a dugout to launch it. But To-mah jabbered at him in Sac, and Joe grunted agreement. I caught the sense of it: Smash holes in all but one dugout, cut off pursuit. Joe hefted a broken chunk of the limestone and raised it.

Before he could bring it down, a howl of rage drifted from the clearing uptrail. Our absence had been noticed. No time now. No time for anything except getting the smallest dugout launched. Between the three of us we managed to drag its pinewood bulk into the water. Joe steadied the craft as we climbed in, then he thrust us off from shore with his foot, leaped into the stern, and grabbed a paddle.

There were paddles to spare. To-mah and I dug in too, and the dugout shot slick as oil through the snaky shadows toward the open river. It rolled wide away before us like a silver spill of moonfrost, whipped choppy by the wind. We'd pulled a good distance downstream before the Winnebagoes reached the shore, their yells mingling with the crack of musket fire.

We ducked our heads and plied our paddles for all we were worth. But the moonlight was tricky; their fuddled condition didn't lend itself to accuracy, either. But then, a musket isn't much good beyond eighty yards, and we were pulling away fast. We were pretty well out of range by the time they got the three remaining craft into the water.

We pressed on steadily for I reckon a mile, holding our

own. Then the balance of musclepower began to tell against us. They were six men to a dugout, we only one man and two boys. At first they'd probably been too drunk to coordinate their paddling, but the liquor was wearing off with exertion and now they were sinking into a smooth rhythm. At this rate we'd be overtaken within minutes.

Our only chance, it looked like, was to put directly into shore and take to the woods. I was about to yell the suggestion when an idea came to me. My feet were braced firmly against what felt like a bundle of blankets. There were three extra paddles in the dugout bottom. I dropped my paddle, pounced on the bundle, and shook it out.

To-mah jabbed me in the back with his paddle. "What are you doing, clumsy?"

"Don't prod me! You'll see. . . ."

I worked quickly, meantime explaining what I had in mind. To-mah grasped it at once, and I saw him grin, I swear, for the first time.

I secured a blanket between two of our paddles, tying the corners to the blades and handles with double knots. Then To-mah and I squirmed into side-by-side positions amidships. We each grasped one of the blanket-tied paddles.

"Now," I said, and we swung the paddles aloft, straining them apart so the blanket snapped taut between them. The idea worked almost too well! The strong wind tore furiously at the improvised sail. It bellied like a balloon, and the paddles were nearly yanked from our hands. It took all our combined strength to hold them erect.

The whole craft surged with the thrust of windpower. Its prow cut the moonlit water like a blade, taking us swiftly south. The angry howls of our pursuers rolled across the water. They resumed shooting. Musket balls plopped the water around us, spouting tiny silver geysers. Luckily their aim hadn't improved; meantime we were drawing gradually out of range again.

We raced on that way for a mile or so. In the stern, Joe Devil Bear made a rudder of sorts with his paddle. We were pulling a slowly increasing lead on the renegades. Either they lacked blankets or hadn't more wit than to rely on human muscle alone. They gave us a hard chase and kept us in sight, but it looked as if the only thing that could upset our escape now was the wind dropping off, which it didn't; it held brisk.

We ran into trouble of a different sort. The upper Mississippi is a maze of channels and islands; Joe Devil Bear's ability to steer the dugout was considerably limited with the craft under sailpower. We'd slipped into a narrowing channel, and suddenly the wind was driving us straight at the hulk of a forested island.

We were quite close to where it divided the channel in two before I told To-mah to lower sail. Then we grabbed up spare paddles and aided Joe's efforts in swinging past the island and down the east channel. Once more the yelling at our back grew louder, the renegades making a last determined attempt to run us down.

The channel narrowed dangerously toward its end, for here the island broadened and almost touched the main shore. Then we shot through the bottleneck and were past the island; the river yawned open again. I gave To-mah the order, and we paddle-hoisted the sail.

We swung it up too fast, was the whole trouble. An unexpected burst of wind grabbed the blanket and almost jerked the paddle from my hands. As it was, my side was yanked askew. Before I could straighten my paddle upright, the wind slapping the half-crumpled sail whipped the craft around sideways. The choppy wind-rough water completed the disaster. The dugout simply rolled over, spilling us into the cold river.

I spluttered up to the surface, almost giving a yell for my companions before good sense choked it off. A moment later both of them surfaced close by me, and I gasped, "To shore —quick. . . ."

We'd capsized not a dozen yards offshore; a few quick strokes pulled us to an overhang of water-trailing willows and osiers that fringed the bank. Seizing hold, we dragged ourselves from the water, then floundered up the bank into the brush. We crouched shivering there, watching the three dugouts shoot into the narrow channel.

They hauled up beside our upended and drifting craft. The renegades pointed at it; they jabbered among themselves. Their anger and disgust were obvious. Whether we'd drowned or had gotten ashore in the dark, they'd lost us. Finally they laid hold of the swamped dugout, maneuvered it to the bank just a few yards below us, and righted it. Several of the Winnebagoes got in and the four dugouts pushed off upchannel, turning back the way they'd come.

We were out of immediate danger, but our situation was far from cozy. I was drenched and numb, my teeth chattering. I jumped up and down, beating my crossed arms against my sides. Joe Devil Bear watched me with mild surprise, To-mah with lip-curled amusement. Both were accustomed to extreme discomfort. I doubt if either had ever caught a cold in his life.

Joe said he could lead us from here to a branch of the Sukisep Trail, from which we could strike straight for Prairie du Chien. So we set out. It was pitch-dark under the trees, hard going through the bogs and brush motts that laced the area. Mosquitoes flourished in these low, swampy, windless places. They preferred me to my companions, and I was kept busy slapping at them. All this activity had one nice effect, which was to keep me warm. In spite of a high wind, the summer night wasn't too chilly, and the pumping heat of my body kept my wet clothes warm on my skin.

Soon we passed onto high-ground prairie and swung south along the broad, moon-splashed trace of the Sukisep Trail. Joe Devil Bear tramped steadily, a man of iron; but I was sore all over, growing tired, my thoughts running together like slow syrup. And To-mah had overused his leg; his limp was getting so bad he could barely hobble. I suggested that we stop for the night.

Joe had flint and steel; he quickly built a fire, and we all squatted around it, soaking up the heat, letting our clothes dry on our bodies. Dry warmth brought drowsiness. To-mah and I stretched out and soon dropped off to sleep.

CHAPTER FOURTEEN

The sun was high when we woke. It was midmorning. Aside from being hungry, sore-muscled, and itchy from mosquito bites, I didn't feel half bad. Joe Devil Bear still squatted in the position he'd been in when I'd dropped off. I didn't have to ask; I knew he'd sat watch all night long. I woke To-mah, and Joe hacked down a sapling and made another crude crutch for him. To-mah tried to proudly disregard it, but changed his mind after he'd taken a few painful steps.

Traveling at an easy pace to accommodate To-mah, we didn't reach Prairie du Chien till early afternoon.

I can't describe the welcome we got. I don't know whether Pa and Mother were more relieved or mad. Mother, who didn't usually carry on, was just about beside herself. Pa held it in a good deal better, but you could tell he'd been shaken up. He'd had cause to be, my overnight disappearance coming right on the heels of an attempt on his life. I'll admit I was most concerned about losing his rifle and my own, but he said not to worry, we'd recover them later.

I told about our adventure, leaving out nothing. This included Henniger's trying to assassinate Pa.

"Well!" Mother said brusquely. She'd had a few minutes in which to collect herself. "I hope that serves you a lesson. Kevin, you should certainly know better than to take so much on yourself . . . you might have confided in your father, if not me. And To-mah, I'm ashamed of you, starting out to . . . the very idea!"

"Yes, ma'am," I said.

To-mah nodded politely. "Yes, lady."

"Nobody tells me anything! And Amos, you're as bad as any boy. If Kev hadn't just told me, I'd never have known."

Pa gave his pipestem a quick, embarrassed swipe across his jaw. "Yes. Well, I didn't see putting you to a lot more worry for no reason. . . ."

"No reason! Being shot at isn't reason enough, I suppose? You march yourself right over to headquarters and tell Sam McRee about those two men."

"I told him," Pa said mildly, "last night when I went to him about Kev and To-mah being missing. I hazarded that Henniger was behind their disappearance, though I had no proof it was he who tried to kill me. It might interest you boys to know that today Captain McRee turned out half the garrison to look for you. But I don't reckon he'll mind when he's heard your story. Come along, we'll see him now."

"They should eat something first," Mother objected.

"Well, you prepare it and we'll be back time it's ready. Joe, you come too, and To-mah."

As we tramped toward the fort's west gate, I said: "Pa, what will happen to Henniger and Valois?"

"I reckon not much. Oh, they'll be convicted for selling whisky to Indians, but the worst penalty that carries is having your trade stores confiscated, your trading license taken away, and a fine levied. The court can order their 'still' destroyed and the furs they got from the Indians seized to cover the fine and court costs. And that's about all."

"But Pa, Henniger tried to kill you! He admitted it to us."

"Your word against his, I'm afraid."

We crossed the parade ground to the captain's office. Captain McRee seemed pleased to see To-mah and me, notwithstanding the inconvenience we'd put him to, and even more pleased to learn that we knew the whereabouts of the whisky traders.

"You fellows think you can lead a squad of soldiers to that cave?"

"Yes, sir!" The anger and dismay I was feeling heated my words. "I just can't see what difference it makes. I can't see bothering to bring 'em in if they're going to be let go again. Maybe so Henniger can get another shot at my pa. . . ."

Pa, just behind me, gave me a hard prod between the shoulders. "Your speech is immoderate, boy," he said. "Curb it."

McRee smiled. "Well, I trust it won't go all that badly, Kevin. It's true the law doesn't swing much of a bludgeon against these illicit traders. But they kidnaped you, there's a solid charge in itself, also one that'll put meat on your testimony that Henniger admitted to attempted murder. That's enough to let me hold 'em without bail till they're arraigned before district court. For the time being, they'll make no more trouble for you Trasks. And afterward—well, if I choose to run such a splendid pair of polecats out of the country, I doubt the civil authorities will object very loudly. Does that satisfy you?"

"Yes, sir."

"Very well. We'd better not delay sending a squad to that cave to collect the evidence. Gray Fox and his friends may have informed Henniger and Valois that you escaped. Possibly, but if they were as drunk as you say, very probably not.

In any case, whether we get the pair of them today or later, they're finished in this territory."

Pa laid one hand on my shoulder, the other on To-mah's. "Sam, I don't think you should count on these two as guides. They're about played out, and I'm sure my good wife will insist they've had enough excitement. No doubt Joe Devil Bear will consent to lead you to the cave. . . ."

And that's how it was. Much as I honed to be on the capture of Henniger and Valois, I didn't object. Pa's easy tone had hinted that the matter was not being opened for discussion, it was settled.

Which, as it turned out, was just as well. For after I'd stowed away a good meal, I found myself quite tired and light-headed. Suddenly I felt as if I could sleep for a week. I went into the tent and stretched out on my bedroll. Before I fell asleep, I heard To-mah limp quietly in and take to his blankets too.

* * *

Actually I only slept about two hours. What roused me was a sound of voices outside the tent. A little groggy with sleep and the day's sticky heat, I left the tent and went out to join Pa and Mother and Ena. They were watching a detachment of troops file up the gravel road leading from the waterfront to the fort gate.

"Are they back already?" I asked.

Pa shook his head. "That's not the squad that went after Henniger and Valois. These troops were sent up the Wisconsin early this morning. You know that after the battle on the Wisconsin Heights, Black Hawk sent his old people and children, his sick and injured, downriver on rafts. Well, a scout brought word the rafts were nearly to the Mississippi, so McRee sent this squad up the Wisconsin in *bateaux* to intercept them."

"How strange," Mother murmured. "I don't see any prisoners."

"There's a few," Pa said. "See, toward the end of the line?"

A few, yes. About a dozen. They were herded along by musket-ready soldiers and they all looked very old, very young, or very sick. But surely there were more than this! The job of making prisoners of a passel of sick, weak people should have been an easy one. What could have happened? There was no air of jubilation about the troops. I can't quite describe how they looked. Faintly sullen, I think. And their martial pride seemed somehow dented and stained.

Pa glanced through the tent flap at the sleeping To-mah. Then he said to me: "Come on, son. Let's go to McRee's office. I'm interested to hear what happened."

We followed the returning troops into the parade ground. Lieutenant Hardy, the crisp young officer who'd led the squad, told his sergeant to dismiss all the men except the guards. Then he walked over to Captain McRee, who was standing on the steps of the headquarters building, staring at the Indians. McRee asked Hardy a sharp question, and the reply didn't satisfy him. He snapped another question.

Hardy's answer caused McRee's face to turn noticeably pale. McRee took a cigar from his lips and dashed it to the ground. By now Pa and I, coming down the long parade crosswalk, were near enough to hear his furious dressing-down of the flushed lieutenant.

"By God, Hardy! I'll have your bars for this!" McRee's voice trembled with shock and fury. "How dare you commit so foul an act in your country's name?"

"Sir," Hardy said with a frozen dignity, "I followed your orders—"

"My orders were to intercept those Indians and bring them here!"

"Sir, you said we were to defend ourselves if fired on."

"You were fired on?"

"Well . . . nobody fired, exactly. We met the rafts at Barrett's Ferry, about twelve miles upriver. As we approached them, I called on the Indians to surrender, and this one old Indian pointed his flintlock at me. In order to prevent his shooting me, I found it necessary—"

"*One* old Indian?" McRee was incredulous. "Because one old man made a threatening *gesture*, you found it necessary to order your men to kill thirty of his companions?"

"No, sir, of course not. I merely gave the command to fire. In proper defense, as you ordered."

McRee groaned. "All right," he said softly. "What happened then?"

"Well, our volley knocked several of the beggars into the water. I assumed the rest would take that as fair warning and give up. Instead—it was unbelievable, Captain—some of those ancient gaffers grabbed up a few rusty muskets they had and started blazing away. So I ordered my troops to fire at will. We dusted several more, and then the rest took to the water, attempting to escape. We picked off a number of them in the water. All this, of course, after they'd been offered the chance to surrender."

"Of course," McRee said in a too-quiet voice. "And then?"

"Sir, some were hit fatally, others seemed unable to swim. These drowned. A few got to shore and escaped into the woods. The remainder we captured, as you can see."

"Yes. The remainder. Tell me, Lieutenant." McRee motioned jerkily at the huddled bunch of Indians. "Why did you take so many alive?"

"Sir?"

"Never mind. Have your men escort these Sacs to the stockade. Have you any wounded?"

"No, sir. We were quite fortunate."

"Then you—you, Mr. Hardy, nobody else—fetch the surgeon.

Some of these Indians have wounds. I want Dr. Beaumont to look at them. On the double!"

Lieutenant Hardy saluted and wheeled away, shouting orders. The captain took another cigar out of his pocket, gazed at it, and then put it away. He seemed to notice Pa and me for the first time.

"Well," he said bitterly, "what do you think of it, Amos?"

"Not much," Pa said. "I could have added some to what you said."

"So could I. What good would it do? You think Mr. Hardy cares even a little? Or that he could care any less?" Shaking his head, McRee walked to his office door. He paused there, glancing at Pa. "They were only Indians. Redskins. Sub-humans. Animals. That's what people like Hardy see, and that's how they treat 'em. Ah no, Amos. No. It wouldn't do any good at all. . . ."

* * *

When To-mah woke a little later, I told him what had occurred at Barrett's Ferry. Not a word from him. Not a flicker of expression. Nor did he take any interest in Henniger and Valois when, toward sunset, they were brought in by the squad that Joe Devil Bear had guided to the cave.

I stood by the fort gate and watched them come in. The two men must have have been taken by surprise, but I guess Henniger had put up a fight. He had a big bruise on his forehead, and his hands were tied behind him. He cussed me viciously as they passed by. Valois seemed to take it very casually, walking between his soldier guards as if he were strolling down a city boulevard. He gave me a jaunty wink as he went by, as if to say it was all part of the game.

Meantime To-mah had slipped away, and now I went looking for him. I found him by the shore of the Wisconsin-Mississippi junction, staring across the water.

"What do you think you're doing?" I asked.

"It's a far way from where the soldiers killed my brothers and sisters," he said. "But the river brings many things from above. Maybe it will bring some of them here."

We saw no bodies then nor during the several days that followed. I suppose they sank before they reached here or would maybe come up later on and be carried along this far. But I never saw any.

* * *

The massacre at Barrett's Ferry was the first of several fast-moving events that brought the Black Hawk War to a bloody close. The next incident came three days later.

From field dispatches, we knew that General Atkinson's Army had been pursuing Black Hawk's main band westward, pressing steadily on their trail. The Sacs had nearly reached the Mississippi. Their likeliest crosspoint would appear to be somewhere between the mouths of two Mississippi tributaries, the Iowa and Bad Axe rivers, some forty miles above Prairie du Chien. So Captain Throckmorton's *Warrior* had been making daily patrols up the Mississippi, on guard against any attempted crossing. Today Throckmorton's vigilance had produced results.

Captain McRee dropped by our tent that evening and glumly told us about it.

This afternoon, it seemed, Throckmorton had spotted a large party of Indians on the east bank about a mile below the Bad Axe. They'd been signaling with a white flag. In the parley that followed, an old Indian who'd claimed he was Black Hawk had requested that the white leader send a boat to bring him and others out to the smoke-belching war canoe so that terms of surrender could be discussed. Throckmorton claimed he'd suspected treachery. In any case, he'd ordered

a load of canister shot fired into the party. It had mowed
down above twenty of the savages. Then he'd steamed back
to Prairie du Chien to refuel and make his report.

"I guess it's no more than you'd expect," Pa said wearily.
"That makes three times Black Hawk tried to surrender. First
before Stillman's Run, then at the Wisconsin Heights, now
today. He got the same answer each time. Why, Sam?"

"I don't know, Amos. Most of us were raised on tales of
Indian treachery and atrocities in the East. Stories like the
Cherry Valley Massacre, passed down from our parents and
grandparents. That, I suppose, is part of it. But I believe some
men would rather kill Indians than eat a good meal. To
them, it's just plain good fun."

To-mah stood by, listening, his face stony. I didn't know
what his thoughts were. He never showed them to white
people, and I was glad of it. Right then I didn't want to
know what he was thinking.

"I've received another dispatch from Atkinson," said McRee.
"He's bringing his troops up with all haste to the mouth of
the Bad Axe. He means to catch Black Hawk between his
lines and the river."

"And then what, Captain?" Mother asked quietly. "Will
they kill all of them?"

"Well, ma'am, from developments so far, I expect we can
look for the worst. Captain Throckmorton will be there
with his *Warrior,* you can bet, and plenty of canister for his
six-pounder. The Sacs will need time to build rafts, and even
if they do—" McRee shrugged. "They'll be caught between
Atkinson on land, Throckmorton on the water."

I listened awhile longer, absorbed by McRee's gloomy
predictions about how the battle would go. Then I noticed
that To-mah was missing again.

Mind, I hadn't been trying to keep an eye on him every

second. It was impossible. Besides, his disappearing for a few minutes didn't necessarily signify anything out of the ordinary.

Not usually. But this time it did. I was as coldly sure of it as I was of my own name. One minute he'd been standing there . . . the next, he was gone. McRee had pinned down within a mile or so the place where the Sacs were expected to try a crossing.

Sure. What else did he need to know?

I moved away from the tents, then broke into a run toward the landing. Dusk was soaking up the last daylight. I saw To-mah ahead of me, crutching along at a furious pace. I overtook him a couple hundred feet from the riverbank and the drawn-up canoes.

Swinging around in front of him, I brought him to a stop.

"You're not going to," I said between my teeth, "so forget it."

"Kevin." He said my name for the first time. "I must do this. Let me go."

"No!" I yelled.

"Tomorrow my people will fight their last battle. They'll sing their death songs and shoot their last arrows. I must go to them, I must be with them. Do you see this?"

"I can't—" I swallowed what I'd started to say. The usual about not setting him free to kill more whites. Words that sank in my throat like clammy stones. After what white men had done. . . . "I won't. Now you turn around and get back!"

"*Cawn*," he said softly. "Friend, let me go."

"No!"

He looked at me a moment longer, then slowly turned and limped back toward the tents. I fell in beside him.

"You've got to see how it is," I told him. "I have a duty to my own, too. It's that against—"

I sensed the bracing of his body. Saw in the dusk a dark

blur that was his crutch sweeping up. I tried to spin away, but too late. The hardwood end fetched me a stunning blow across the forehead.

Next I knew, I was down on my hands and knees, red sunbursts exploding in my head. I was that way for just a second or so, it seemed. Yet when I raised my head, To-mah had already reached the riverbank. He was shoving one of the beached canoes into the water.

I got painfully to my feet, feeling a hot wetness jet down my forehead. I touched it and looked at the glistening smear on my hand. Blood, but not much. I lurched toward the landing at a stumbling run.

To-mah had climbed into the canoe and snatched up a paddle. I slogged in after the craft, stumbled, and fell to my knees, splashed back to my feet, and lunged on. I hit a drop-off, water surging suddenly from my knees to my hips.

But I grabbed wildly and hooked the canoe's prow with my fingertips. Then I dug in my heels and started to back out of the water, pulling the canoe with me.

I expected To-mah to take a swing at me with the paddle or his crutch, though it would be an awkward attempt at best, and I was ready for it. But he didn't do anything. Didn't say anything. Just sat and watched me tug him back to captivity.

Two feet from the bank, I came to an abrupt stop in the water. The woolly dusk blurred To-mah's face, but what did it matter? He never let you see anything in it.

"What do you want from me?" I yelled at him. "What?"

Still he said nothing. He'd given his answer, and there was no more to say. And suddenly I couldn't think about it any more. I was done with thinking.

I jammed my foot against the prow and thrust with all my strength. The canoe shot outward, and then the current caught it.

"Go on!" I shouted. "Blast you, go on, get out of here!"

A paddle dipped, water rustled. The craft wheeled slowly upriver. In a minute it was lost to sight in the crooked sway of water shadows.

CHAPTER FIFTEEN

Pa grumbled some about paying off the irate owner of one more lost canoe. Mother sewed up the cut in my forehead with stout thread and put on a bandage. Telling them roughly how To-mah had escaped, I omitted to mention that I might have stopped him. I doubt that they'd have blamed me any, but I wasn't sure I'd done the right thing. As I said, I didn't want to think about it.

But in my blankets that night, I couldn't keep from thinking. I lay awake a long time. I wondered if To-mah would reach his people in time to satisfy his big wish. It was a long way to the Bad Axe, but if he paddled like fury all night, he should get there sometime tomorrow. In my thoughts I called him a fool for being in such a hurry to throw his life away. But I didn't really feel that way. I'd have done the same, I reckon.

Cawn, he had said. Friend. Maybe he had slicked me up to soften me, but I didn't believe that either. We'd been thrown together for weeks and had pulled through a tight situation together. No matter how a fellow starts out feeling, the way things happen can force some big changes in him.

Early next morning, the *Warrior* steamed her way upriver again. She left before sunrise, but I was already up. I stood in the gray light and watched till she'd disappeared. It gave me a chill to think about what that canister-firing six-pounder on her deck would do to human flesh. One minute I wished I'd gone with To-mah to help in his fight; next minute I cussed myself for being as big a fool as he.

In the end, I didn't hope for either a white or Indian victory. For no matter who lost this war, there'd be no winner.

It was a long day. A quiet fever of excitement ran through the village. Everyone knew that the final clash between Black Hawk and the Army was on. We were all sure of the outcome, yet we were all on needles waiting for news.

It didn't reach us till next morning, when the *Warrior* chugged into the landing. Aboard her were General Henry Atkinson, Colonel Zachary Taylor, Governor John Reynolds of Illinois, and a number of prominent officers in the Illinois and Michigan militias. Within minutes, word of their arrival had spread through Prairie du Chien.

It was all a fellow could do to sort the facts from the rumors, but I was pretty sure of one thing. Captain McRee's worst expectations had come about. It had been fully as bad as he'd predicted, and then some.

I didn't know how much to believe of all I heard, but from what I was able to verify later, it had gone something like this. The Sacs hadn't finished building their rafts when scouts had reported the arrival of General Atkinson's Army. The canny Black Hawk had sent out a decoy war party to meet Atkinson's force and draw it north, leading the troops several miles upstream above the intended crossing. Militia Brigadier James Henry, figuring out the ruse, had discovered the main band and attacked it, but not before the Indians had gotten some of the rafts launched. Atkinson's troops, warned by a messenger from Henry, had arrived in time to help in the fight. Or slaughter. Though weak from hunger and disease, the Sac warriors had fought a furious rear-guard action to cover the retreat of their women and children by raft.

Then the *Warrior* had arrived on the scene. It had sprayed the rafts with bursts of canister, killing many Indians outright and wrecking the rafts. Scores of wounded had drowned. Those trying to swim to a nearby island had been picked off by riflemen.

The final mopping-up was done with a bayonet charge. The troops had swarmed across the shoreline, cleaning out the last pockets of resistance. Then they'd waded out to the island and wiped out every Indian who'd taken refuge there, regardless of sex, age, or physical condition. The irregulars, or militiamen, had then indulged a favorite pastime of removing redskin scalps, while others tore strips of skin from the backs of dead Indians to be cured for razor straps.

The slaughter had gone on for three hours, more or less. About a dozen whites had been killed, a dozen more wounded. At least 150 Indians had been killed and around an equal number had drowned when the *Warrior* had fired into the rafts. Somebody allowed that it had been a terrible thing that so many women and kids had been shot "by accident." Governor Reynolds, who wasn't known to favor our red brethren, was heard to remark that "the conflict resembled a carnage more than a regular battle."

All that day bunches of militiamen kept straggling in. Weary men, bone-gaunt and bearded, some of them were exultant, some silent. The taprooms opened early this day, and celebrations went on far into the night. In a few days they'd all be mustered out and homeward bound. Now they just wanted to relax, drink, and brag it up. I guess they figured they'd earned it.

We Trasks were anxiously waiting some word of Theron. Surely he'd come to Prairie du Chien, for he'd known of Pa's plan to wait out the war here. We scanned all the incoming groups, watching for Ther or anyone who might have news of him. I was all over the village, keeping eyes and ears open.

It wasn't till sunset that Pa and I spotted some Blue River volunteers, among them Bob Yarnell and Buck Tolliver. We lost no time questioning them.

"I wisht I could tell you some'at, Mr. Trask," Tolliver said. "But we all got mixed up in that big battle, and afterward the companies never did muster back together. We seen Ther just before the fight—him and Ceph Mangrum was right beside us, wa'n't they, Bob?—but I ain't saw hide nor hair of 'em since."

"They are likely helping guard the prisoners," Yarnell assured us. "There's a big passel of redskins being herded down the Sukisep Trail. Reckon they should get here sometime tomorrow."

But Pa was worried, Mother and Ena no less so when they'd been told. And I had room in my thoughts for To-mah too. Had he gotten in on the big battle? Had he come through it alive?

* * *

A slow rain began to fall before dawn broke next day. I sat inside the tent all morning and stared out the open flap, watching heavy drops stitch the puddles with little geysers. It was still drizzling when the survivors of Black Hawk's band were marched in from the north, shortly before noon. Pa and I muffled ourselves against the weather as well as we could, then went out to see if Ther was among the militia guards.

Anxious as I was about my brother, seeing the Sac captives nearly wiped everything else from my mind. I didn't want to look, yet couldn't tear my eyes away. Pa was affected the same way. We stood in the dismal rain and watched columns of them file by toward the stockade. They were wasted to skin and bone, more like walking skeletons than people.

We didn't learn till later, when the Indians had told their side, exactly how they'd fared these last weeks. Harried by troops, kept constantly on the move, they'd lived on snatches of food. When the last cracked corn was gone, the last gaunt horses killed for eating, they'd resorted to berries and acorns, grass and bark, roots and insects. Dozens had died of starvation and exhaustion.

Many showed the effects of disease and badly tended wounds. Women were wailing with grief, arms and legs covered with gashes, faces and hair smeared with dirt, and I knew this was how they mourned their dead. I noticed how few babies there were and wondered if a lot of them had died.

I looked for To-mah, but couldn't see him anywhere. And then I couldn't look any longer.

"Pa! Pa! Kev! . . ."

If I hadn't known that voice to be Theron's, I'd have sworn at first it was a dirty, scraggly-bearded stranger coming toward us. He was terribly thin, his clothes flapping in tatters. His skin was weathered a deep russet color, and he was limping a little.

He dropped his musket and ran the last few yards, and grabbed hold of Pa. I thought that Ther might start to bawl, but that was never his style. He just held onto Pa a minute, then gave me a bearhug, and I swear *I* almost choked up.

Cephas Mangrum was tramping our way too, grinning broadly. He looked even more fine-worn than Ther, and spots of fever burned in his cheeks. Then I realized that Rowena was beside us, a shawl hugged around her shoulders, the rain matting her pale hair. I saw Ceph look at her. His smile faded, his walk slowed. He was wearing a heavy-weave blanket, greased to turn rain, around his upper body. He threw it back to show his right arm in a sling. The hand was gone, the stump of his wrist bandaged.

Rowena cried, "Ceph, Ceph!" and ran to him. He should have known my sister better than to think a missing hand would matter. But I didn't think he'd forget after today.

We returned to the tents. Mother shed a few tears before she ladled out cups of hot beef broth for Theron and Ceph. Ther didn't have much to say after the greetings. I couldn't read behind his face, but he was different somehow. I guess we all felt it, but nobody pressed him.

Ceph told us how he'd lost his hand at the tail end of the Bad Axe fight. A musket ball accidentally fired by one of his own comrades had shattered the bone. The surgeon at a field hospital had had no choice but to amputate.

"Could have been worse," Ceph said cheerfully. "Give me time, I'll learn to manage fine one-handed." And you knew he would.

Theron was staring into his cup. "Pa," he said.

"Yes?"

"I found out what you tried to tell us about war. It's just what you said. No glory. No sense to it, even. Two days ago I watched friends of mine do things I still can't believe. And I thought that *Indians* were bloody savages—"

"It's not them, it's not us," Pa broke in gruffly. "War brutalizes all men the same way. Don't let yourself brood on it or it will turn you sour. But don't ever forget it."

Ceph turned the talk to an easier vein, telling us how Captain Marcus Wynant had given what few of his company he could still muster a little speech following what he'd termed "this glorious victory," telling them they'd made the country safe for decent people. "He will run for the territorial legislature on the basis of his powerful leadership," Ceph chuckled. "You wait and see if he doesn't."

"I reckon a good many political reputations will be built on 'this glorious victory,'" Pa said dryly. "I understand the troops failed to capture Black Hawk."

"Yes, sir. Seems he slipped through our hands at the last minute. We did learn that he and a few of his friends and their families escaped toward the east. Colonel Taylor sent a company in pursuit of him, but chances are he'll give 'em the slip. He's got plenty of friends among the tribes who'll be glad to help him. . . ."

* * *

But Black Hawk, it seemed, had run clean out of friends. Next morning he and his followers were brought in by a party of Winnebagoes led by One-Eyed Decori and Chaetar.

These two prominent headmen had been friends of the Hawk's until Joseph Street, U. S. Agent of Indian Affairs, had threatened to cut off the treaty money the government paid their tribe every year. In order to regain favor with their White Father, the Winnebagoes had gone to the Wisconsin Dells, where they knew Black Hawk had taken refuge. The Dells were a maze of caves, ravines, and chimney rocks carved from the sandstone bluffs ages ago by the Wisconsin River. When he'd seen his good friends coming, Black Hawk had emerged from hiding to greet them. They had seized and bound him and brought him to Prairie du Chien.

Colonel Zachary Taylor made quite an occasion of Black Hawk's arrival. He ordered Fort Crawford's garrison to turn out on the parade ground in full dress uniform, and here he and Mr. Street greeted Black Hawk's captors as they entered the fort gates with the Sac leader.

Decori and Chaetar had also captured his son Whirling Thunder and the fanatical medicine man White Cloud, better known as The Prophet. These three men, along with Black Hawk's fiery lieutenant, Neapope, who'd been taken earlier, were the key figures among the Sac rebels. All were big robust men—except Black Hawk himself. I was surprised to see how old, how small and shrunken, he looked.

With these prisoners in hand, the Black Hawk War was ended, the red man's power east of the Mississippi broken forever. It was an historic moment, and Colonel Taylor and Mr. Street made the most of it. Black Hawk's humiliation was complete, yet he rose to the occasion with a stirring speech. I'll never forget the last words.

"I loved my town, my corn fields, the home of my people," he said. "I fought well for them, and my children are not ashamed of me. Now I break the war arrow and take the white man's road. It is finished."

Colonel Taylor spoke briefly, saying that General Atkinson had departed for St. Louis on the *Warrior* shortly before word came of Black Hawk's capture. However, the general had left instructions that covered this event. The old Sac would be sent south to Jefferson Barracks in Missouri, where he'd be confined till the government had decided on his fate. Forty of his followers, including all known members of his family, would be sent with him. The troop escort would be under the command of Lieutenant Robert Anderson, and they'd depart tomorrow morning on the steamboat *Winnebago*.

Standing to one side with other civilian onlookers, I hardly listened to what the colonel was saying.

Where, I wondered, was To-mah? I hadn't seen them bring in Black Hawk, whose fellow captives had already been taken to the stockade. Could the boy I knew as his grandson have been among them? Or had I missed him in yesterday's bunch? Or—could he have been killed in the battle?

Somehow I could not believe it.

CHAPTER SIXTEEN

Standing on a birch knoll some distance above the river-bank, I watched the soldiers urge their human cargo aboard the *Winnebago*. The Sacs had been herded in a shuffling column from the prison stockade south of the fort, and now they were filing up the boat's plank. I counted an even forty: all leading Sac warriors along with their women and children. I couldn't identify To-mah among them, but I was standing pretty far away.

A brisk wind blew; red flakes of sunrise danced on the river. The lieutenant in charge of the detail was standing by the plank, his back to me, giving an order now and then. Well, I told myself, what are you waiting for? Go and ask him.

He couldn't do any worse than refuse me, as the stockade guards had refused Pa and me yesterday.

I'd still hoped against hope that To-mah was among the survivors brought in. So with Pa's help, I'd tried to get a look inside the stockade itself. Together we'd approached the log enclosure, only to be turned back by Army sentries. Nobody was to go near the prisoners, we were told. Order of

Colonel Taylor. As the colonel was Pa's friend, I'd thought he might make an exception in our case. But Taylor would want an explanation, Pa pointed out. That would mean telling him we'd harbored an enemy, To-mah, in time of war. A fact to which the colonel wouldn't take kindly at all.

So I'd come down near the landing this early dawn, hoping to find To-mah among the Sac captives being sent to Jefferson Barracks. Or, failing that, getting a chance to ask one of these Indians if he knew anything about To-mah's fate.

It all depended on the temper of Lieutenant Anderson. We'd never met, though I knew him by sight. If he was feeling indulgent, he might just oblige me. Even if he wouldn't, I could get a closer look at the Indians. I walked down to the bank and came up behind the officer.

"Sir—" I started to say.

He turned, and it wasn't Lieutenant Anderson. I recognized this fellow as Lieutenant Jefferson Davis, the young Southerner whom Zachary Taylor had introduced as his aide. We'd met only that once, months ago, but he smiled his recognition.

"Let's see . . . Trask, isn't it?"

"Yes, sir. Kevin Trask. Glad you remember me."

"Of course. You, your father, two brothers. How are all of them?"

I told him briefly about Ben's death and the situation that had brought us to Prairie du Chien, also that we planned to start back to our Blue River farm today. Lieutenant Davis said he was sorry to hear about Ben.

"Sir," I said, "I thought Lieutenant Anderson was taking Black Hawk and the others downriver."

"Anderson took sick last night. Touch of the cholera, but apparently not serious. I'm assigned to take his place."

"I wonder . . ." I looked offhandedly at the boat's lower deck, the apathetic Indians and the soldiers with muskets standing at regular intervals along the rail. "You think I could go aboard a minute? I'd like to palaver with one of those Indians."

Davis grinned. "One in particular, or will any of 'em do?"

As I ran my eye across the lower deck, I stopped on a familiar face. To-mah! He was gazing straight at me, but gave no sign that he recognized me.

"That one," I said, pointing. "I'd like to talk to that fellow right there."

"Hm. What makes you think he speaks English?"

"Oh, I talk Sac middling well. Just a little," I added hastily as the lieutenant gave me a keen look.

"Is this just curiosity, Mr. Trask, or what?"

"Curiosity," I said. "He's about my age, wouldn't you say?"

"Can't you talk from here?"

"I'd kind of like a personal word with him, sir."

Lieutenant Davis eyed me a long moment. A sparkle of mischief touched his smile. I had the feeling he'd broken a rule or two himself when he was my age. "Well," he said, "I can't see any harm in it. We cast off in a few minutes, so you'd better hustle."

I hurried up the plank. The soldiers had seen Davis pass me aboard, so they let me by without comment. To-mah looked unconcernedly at the sky until I was squarely in front of him. Then he lowered his gaze to me and said: "You took long enough."

I had to remind myself that he was just naturally too cross-grained not to make a prickly comment. I noticed the blood-stained rag tied around his forearm. "You're lucky I came at all," I said. "For someone who *claims* to be Black Hawk's grandson, you're mighty hard to find."

This touched his pride like hot iron. He straightened on his crutch, his eyes sparking. "Come!" he said sharply.

He led the way to the starboard rail above the paddle-wheel housing where one Indian stood by himself, gazing across the river—a small old man wrapped in a blanket, his plucked scalp gleaming like a copper dome. Silver bangles rimmed each of his ears. His face was gaunt and sunken-cheeked, yet the skin stretched taut and unlined across its bones. At sixty-five, Black Hawk looked bent and battered by trouble, not by time.

"My grandfather," To-mah said with soft respect.

"My grandson," answered Black Hawk. "Is this the *Muc-a-mon* who was your friend?"

"This is he. His father and his mother are not here, but as he is, so they are. They should belong to the Yellow Earth People, Grandfather. Their hearts are good."

Black Hawk's fine mouth almost smiled. "That is not what you have learned. Gitchee-Manitou has put good hearts in some white skins as he put bad hearts in some *A-saw-we-ke* skins. That is what you have learned."

I followed the meat of this exchange in Sac, but what could I say? I felt awed. This was the Indian who'd offered my country the toughest challenge it had faced in twenty years, forced thousands of white troops and militia to take the field against him, outwitted our best military minds again and again. All this because Black Hawk and his people prized what the people they fought prize above all else. Something without which Americans would not be Americans. And that was freedom.

To-mah drew me down the rail a short distance. "Now do you believe?"

"I never doubted," I grinned. "I just like to be shown." I pointed at his arm. "Did you get hurt?"

"It is nothing. A scratch. Made by a white man who shoots as badly as you. Do you have a knife?"

"Sure."

"I have no knife."

Well, it wasn't that I fancied giving up my treasured case-

knife, but what do you say when it's put to you just that way?
A friend is a friend, even if he has a rude way of asking.
I took the knife from my pocket and handed it to him. He
opened the large blade.

"Hey!" I said.

"Hold out your arm," he said, smiling a little.

He'd given his own right arm a short, clean slash above the
wrist. Now I understood, and I rolled up my sleeve and lifted
my right arm. He made a quick cut corresponding to his
own. We gripped one another's elbows, and our blood ran
together and dripped on the deck.

"The Manitou is witness that we two are brothers," To-mah
said in his own tongue. "No matter where we go, how far in
time and place, the blood of our bodies is one and we are
one."

He wiped the knife clean and held it out.

"It is yours," I said.

He shook his head, thoughtfully. "I have nothing to give
in return. There will be another time. Keep it awhile."

I thought he'd given plenty, but I took back the knife and
returned it to my pocket. And then Lieutenant Davis was calling me to hurry, it was time to cast off. I muttered something
to To-mah, I don't recall what, and hurried off the boat.

Lieutenant Davis gave me an amused and speculative look.
Plain enough there'd been more than mere curiosity behind
my wish to board the boat. "Quite a talk you had," he observed. "You hurt your arm, I see."

I pressed my left hand over the slash. "I must have cut it,"
I said.

To-mah was standing by the rail. We looked at each other,
but said nothing as the moorings were cast off, the plank
hauled in. The *Winnebago*'s twin stacks belched smoke, and
she pulled away as the red dawn brilliance softened to topaz.

"*Cawn!*" To-mah called suddenly. "*Si-say!*"

Friend. Brother. I grinned, and answered him by raising my hand.

And he grinned back.